GIRL COUNTRY

"*Girl Country* is a stunner. The stories here enthrall, and the characters pulse with life. Stories that tantalize and elude and haunt. These are the stories of a confident writer in absolute control of her art, rendered in a gracious, delightful prose. A striking collection by a powerful new voice."

—Brad Felver, author of *The Dogs of Detroit*

"Alongside the Jersey Devil and the ghost haunting Jenny Jump Mountain, add the voice of Vogtman to the list of strange magic coming out of New Jersey. Vogtman's *Girl Country* is a wondrously inventive journey through the monstrous landscapes women and girls must navigate, and an inquisitive, visceral, and often funny exploration of the monsters that dwell in every woman. *Girl Country* takes its reader from the present to the past and far into the future, with a wisdom and prescience that makes the collection both timely and utterly timeless. A stunning debut from an unforgettable writer."

—Bess Winter, author of *Machines of Another Era*

"Vogtman's debut could not have come at a more prescripted time. Her stories of lost, damaged souls offered a second chance—be it with a strange girl found on the side of the road, a busload of refugees heading north, or an unwanted child thrust into their arms—sketch vulnerable everybodies seeking redemption in a world that's been unkind, unrelenting, and unreal. Vogtman is skilled at finding these pilgrims at the perfect moment, thrusting them into make-or-break opportunities, surprising us with each and every tale. This is a heartbreaking and powerful debut from a writer with impressive powers."

—Michael Czyzniejewski, author of *The Amnesiac in the Maze*

GIRL
COUNTRY

GIRL
COUNTRY

— *Stories* —

JACQUELINE VOGTMAN

DZANC
BOOKS

2580 Craig Rd.
Ann Arbor, MI 48103
www.dzancbooks.org

Library of Congress Cataloging-in-Publication Data Available Upon Request

ISBN: 9781950539765
First US edition: May 2023
Interior design by Michelle Dotter
Cover design by Steven Seighman

Grateful acknowledgment is made to the editors of the publications in which the following stories first appeared (some in slightly different form):

"Girl Country," *Mud Season Review*
"Once Bound for Earth," *Kestrel: A Journal of Literature and Art*
"Children and Other Artifacts," *The Lifted Brow*
"A Love Letter From Very Far Away," *Nelle*
"When the Tree Grows This High" (as "The Trees They Grow So High"), *Permafrost*
"BI6FOOT," *Third Coast*
"The Hall of Human Origins," *Prism Review*
"Wilder Family," *Sierra Nevada Review*
"Jubilee Year," *Relief: A Journal of Art and Faith*
"The Mermaid and the Pornographer," *Berkeley Fiction Review*
"The Preservation of Objects Lost at Sea," originally published in *The Emerson Review* and republished in *The Literary Review*

Printed in the United States of America

10   9   8   7   6   5   4   3   2   1

CONTENTS

For my girl, Margot

GIRL COUNTRY

THE FARMER WAS DRIVING a deserted county road in the early darkness of fall when he found the girl. He was on the way home from burying his wife. His brother sat in the passenger seat, and it was he who spotted the girl first: a shape moving on the side of the road, white nightgown, white teeth, whites of the eyes.

"Slow down," the farmer's brother said, and then the farmer saw her too. She kept close to the tree line. When she noticed their truck she ran away, back into the woods. They pulled over.

"We should get her," the farmer's brother said. "See what's wrong."

The farmer sighed. "You go," he said. "I'm tired."

His brother opened the door, and then the farmer thought better of it.

"I'll do it," he said. "You stay here."

The farmer clicked on the flashers and walked into the woods. He looked around, the darkness punctuated every few seconds by a pulse of orange glow. How would he find her? Why was he even looking? His mind was foggy. In the last few weeks of his wife's dying he had not slept. And then to get through the burial this evening, he had drained the flask of whiskey his brother had brought. He was about to turn and walk back to the truck when he heard a twig break and saw a flash of white.

"You okay?" he called after the girl. "You need help?"

The girl stopped running, though she did not turn around.

"We're not gonna hurt you," the farmer said.

The girl turned around, and he saw her face. So much younger than he had thought. Dark hair wild, uncombed, studded with leaves.

"We can help you," he said. He knelt down, opened his hands like coaxing a frightened dog.

She walked toward him but kept her distance, stopping about a dozen feet away. When he turned to walk back toward the road, he could hear the slightest crunch of leaves behind him, following.

When they got to the truck, he asked the girl where she came from, where she was going. She did not answer. She was shaking as she huddled between them in the cab. The brothers looked at each other. Neither of them suggested going to the police; lately it seemed that lost girls got more lost when the cops picked them up.

The farmer looked down at the girl's feet, bare and dirty and cut up. The hospital? Hospitals these days were overloaded with the dying, the last decade seeing an exponential spike in cancer diagnoses, young and old and middle aged all falling ill with new mutations of blood and bone, livers and kidneys and colons. The doctors wouldn't waste a minute on a girl with bloody feet.

"I got too many mouths to feed already," the farmer's brother said. "And you know Nance would never let me bring this girl home."

The farmer's jaw tightened. He thought of his house, silent and empty. He thought of the farm, falling to ruin. He thought of all the days ahead leading to winter, the shorn field, empty like the house. He started the engine and drove.

꙳

The farmer's name was Noah. He was among the last of the small farmers. Factory farms had all but driven them to extinction, but there were still a few old holdouts in the Midwest refusing to let go of their land. Noah knew, however, that it was only a matter of time. With his wife gone, and their one child also dead from cancer at the age of sixteen, and with his bones aching more every day, he knew he could not keep farming long.

When he pulled up to his house after dropping off his brother, the windows were dark and the porch light was out. He led the girl by the hand so she wouldn't trip. At first she jerked back like his touch was flame, but he told her again that he was not going to hurt her. He held his hand out, palm up, until she gingerly touched it and they made their slow way through the darkness. He opened the door. He never locked it, even though crime had risen in tandem with the cancer rate. People didn't fear the cops as much when death was right around the corner.

He turned on the lamp and looked around: the couch where his wife lay, every night, tartan blanket wrapped around her skeletal body, until she needed a bedpan and IVs full of drugs and her bodily fluids were leaking everywhere, at which point she had to be moved to the special hospital-issued bed in the room that used to be their daughter's.

It was late, but the girl would need a bath before she slept. Noah led her to the stairs, and with some coaxing, she followed. He showed her the bathroom, but she did not enter, simply peered in at it like she had never seen a bathroom before. He started the bath for her. He poured shampoo under the running water to make bubbles, like he used to do for his daughter. When the tub was filled, he left her in the bathroom with the door closed and went downstairs to fix himself a sandwich. He made one for the girl too.

When he returned to the bathroom and knocked on the door, there was no answer. Then the girl opened the door. When he peeked in, he saw that she was still standing where he had left her, fully clothed and dirty.

"Don't you want to take a bath?" he asked. He sat down and stirred his hand in the water. "It's warm."

She approached the water and dipped her hand in.

"Yes," he said. "Now just get undressed and sit in the tub, and you can wash yourself with soap, like this."

He took the bar of soap and rubbed it between his hands, lathering. She followed suit, and then splashed her hands in the water. When she took them out, she looked at them with fascination. And then she smiled.

Seeing her smile made him smile too. It had been so long since he'd done it that the sensation felt strange on his face. He left again, and when he came back after eating his sandwich he found her sitting in the tub, arms hugging her knees, hair still dirty and full of leaves. He turned around so his back was to the girl and asked if she needed help washing her hair. No answer. So he turned again, and, feeling less ashamed because the bubbles covered most of her body, he sat by the tub and tilted the girl's head back. He lathered shampoo into her hair, pulling out the leaves and small twigs, pinching off the bloated ticks that were stuck in her scalp. He poured cup after cup of water over her head, and it seemed with each pour she relaxed further, until by the end her head lay heavy against his hand, the weight of it in his muscle memory so much like his daughter's. He used to give his daughter baths up until she was about the girl's age, when his wife said it was no longer appropriate, as she would soon become a woman. And their daughter did become a woman, for a few years at least, until her womanhood turned against her and she developed melon-sized tumors on her ovaries and she was dead within a year. It had been one kind of grief to have his previous three children die during childbirth or within the first few weeks of life—this was common in their country now, and everyone had their theories about why: chemicals in the water, pesticides on the plants, pollution in the air, viruses or immunizations, mutations from the medication most people were on to stave off depression, anxiety, pain, all the rest of life's afflictions. But it was another kind of grief to have raised a child and watched her grow, taught her to farm and cook and play catch, to have read her storybooks at night and made her breakfast in the morning, to have sat on the couch with her and her mother at night watching old TV shows, to have held her while she cried over all the things that kids cry over as they grow up—the consciousness of death, the breaking up of friendships and first loves, the realization that some people had so much and other people had so little—and then, to lose her.

He raised the girl's head from the water and dried it with a towel. Then he took the edge of the towel and dipped it in the water and cleaned her face. It was not his daughter's face after all.

꙳

The next morning, Noah was up early to harvest the corn. He drove the combine through the field for a few hours and then took a break midmorning. He thought he should be there when the girl woke up. When he went into the house, he found her at the sink, washing dishes left over from the previous night.

"You don't have to do those," he said. "Sit down, I'll make you something to eat."

The girl looked as if he had woken her from a dream, and she dropped the plate she'd been holding. He rushed over. The girl tried to pick up the pieces, but he led her to the table and pulled out a chair. She sat, and he cleaned up the broken dish. He then toasted some bread and fried an egg. He put it in front of her, and immediately she began stuffing the food into her mouth.

"Where are you from?" Noah asked. "What's your name?"

She didn't answer. Then he had an idea. He found a pen and the back of a medical bill, and he placed the items in front of her.

"Maybe you could write your name?"

The girl took the pen in her hand. At least she knew how to hold it. That was a good sign. But on the paper, she did not write her name. Instead, she began drawing pictures. Not stick figures exactly, but childish drawings of people. One noticeable trait most of the people in these drawings shared was a protruding midsection. As Noah looked at the drawings, he realized they must be pregnant women.

"Are those women having babies?" he asked. He stuck his abdomen out, pantomiming a ballooning belly. "Did you live with a lot of pregnant women?"

She nodded her head. They were getting somewhere. But what did it mean that she lived with a lot of pregnant women? Was it some kind of commune? A cult?

Noah got another piece of paper. On this, the girl drew the same women, but this time she drew very large breasts on the women, with wavy lines emerging from the breasts.

"Were the women you lived with breastfeeding?" He pantomimed holding a baby to his chest. "Were they nursing their babies?"

She shook her head yes and then no. He got her another piece of paper.

The next picture she drew was harder to understand. Here were the women, some of them pregnant, all of them with extremely large breasts, but attached to those breasts were thin lines leading to a rectangular structure.

"What is that?" he asked.

The girl kept drawing, page after page, until the table was covered in paper.

"I'm sorry," Noah said, shaking his head. "I just don't understand."

❧

Noah spent the rest of the day on the combine, and then after dinner he tried again to talk to the girl. When after a half hour she still didn't speak, he sat with her on the couch and watched TV. It was an old show that had originally aired when he was about her age, over fifty years ago: a comedy called *Mork and Mindy*. In the opening credits, the alien Mork emerges from an egg. This elicited from the girl the first sound he heard her make: laughter. It was childish and bubbled up from deep inside her, and it made him laugh, too. It reminded him of when his daughter was a baby, how every first thing was a miracle. Her first smile, her first laugh. He remembered her first laugh. It was a hot summer day, and they were lying on a blanket in the back yard, having a picnic. His wife was worried the baby was getting too warm, so he blew on his daughter's face, ruffling her wisp of hair, and she giggled for the first time ever. Over twenty years ago, and he still remembered the sound.

The girl fell asleep on the couch near midnight, so Noah had to carry her to bed. He put her in the spare bedroom because the room that his wife and daughter had died in was too full of the scent of death. The spare bedroom lived up to its name: just a bed and a night table, curtains, and a pale imprint on the wall where the crucifix used to hang. Folded at the foot of the bed were some clothes for the girl, his daughter's old clothes. The girl was light, but still his bones ached as he carried her upstairs and bent down to put her in the bed. He was out of breath. He had not been to the doctor in quite a few years, not out of fear but because between his daughter and his wife he was so sick of hospitals, not to mention it was almost impossible to get an appointment these days and so damn expensive when you did. He figured if he were dying, there was nothing he could do about it anyway.

When he went back downstairs, he looked again at the pictures that the girl had drawn. In the last one, the women looked like they were hooked up to some kind of machine. Something about it looked familiar to him. He stared out the open window at the dark field, inhaling the scent of the neighbor's wood-burning stove. In the distance, a cow lowed. He looked down at the paper again and it dawned on him: the picture the girl had drawn reminded him of the machines that his brother used at his dairy farm. The women in these pictures were hooked up to milking machines.

❧

The next morning, Noah spent just two hours harvesting corn, and when the girl was up, he put his work aside and drove her to his brother's farm about five miles away. His brother's name was Zeke. Younger by six years, Zeke had fared a little better than Noah in those things one measured a man's life by: a larger house, three living children, a healthy wife, and a dairy farm that was as close as it could be to thriving, mostly due to the fact that middle-class people were willing to pay good money for organic milk in the hopes that it might help protect them from the cancer epidemic. Wealthy people, of course, no longer drank milk.

During the ride, the girl sat silent beside him. She still hadn't uttered a word, but in most other respects she seemed fine—healthy and able to understand him.

"We're going to see my brother," he told the girl. "Is that okay?"

She nodded and looked at him. Her eyes were dark as soil.

When they got to the farm, Noah found his brother behind the cow shed.

"How is she?" Zeke asked, his voice low. "She talk yet?"

"Not yet. But I got her to draw me a picture."

Noah took the drawing out from his back pocket and showed it to his brother. The girl kept her distance behind them.

"What the fuck?" Zeke grabbed the paper from Noah's hand.

"What do you see in that picture?"

"I see a bunch of titties. Looks like your girl has a dirty mind."

"Look again. Look at this." Noah pointed to the lines coming out of the women's breasts, the rectangles the lines were attached to. "What does it remind you of?"

Zeke looked closer, and then uttered: "Shit. It's a bunch of women getting milked."

"Yeah, that's what I thought," Noah said. "I don't know what to make of it."

Zeke whistled, long and low. "You've never heard?"

"Never heard what?"

"I forgot you're so damn old you don't go on the internet. Boy, have I got a story for you."

❧

"Listen," Zeke said. "This is the stuff of legend. You see things online, and people talk about it in the bar. I've always considered it bullshit and haven't even thought of it in a couple years, but that picture reminded me. Anyway. It was probably about ten years ago, there were these conspiracies popping up online. About how rich people never got sick anymore. Or how, even if they got sick, they had some kind of antidote that cured them and made them live longer. It all seemed pretty basic to me: rich people got better healthcare and better health in general because they're eating organic and vegan and all that. But these conspiracy theory guys, you know, the *eat the rich* types, they're saying it's something else. Some kind of secret serum. And that it's only being given to the rich and famous and powerful, because they want all us poor peons to die off, since basically our population is a drain on the earth."

"You're right," Noah said. "That does sound like bullshit."

They had stopped in front of the milking parlor. Zeke peeked in at his cows attached to the milking machine.

"Hear me out. The secret ingredient, supposedly, is breast milk. Not just the regular kind, but the stuff they call *liquid gold*, the colostrum that comes from a woman right after she gives birth. And this serum is super potent because they give these women drugs or hormones, so when those rich people drink it or inject it, they don't get sick, and they don't age, and they don't die. I mean, they die, but at least not at the rate we're going."

"That's ridiculous." Noah pulled his jacket tighter around himself despite the sun. They kept walking past the milking parlor. The girl was still trailing them by a dozen feet, out of listening range.

"Sure, I thought so, too," Zeke continued. "But the other part of this story is that there are whole farms of women, hidden farms, factories where they hook women up to machines and use them for milk, like cows."

"Where would these women even come from?"

"I don't know. Kidnapped? Prostitutes maybe?"

From behind them, they heard the girl cry out. She was standing in front of the milking parlor, looking in at the cows. She rushed into the building. Noah rushed after her.

"What's the matter?" Noah asked.

"Mama," the girl said, pointing at the cows.

❧

Over the next few weeks, Noah would ask the girl a couple times a day if she wanted to talk, what her name was, and if she could tell him where she came from. She never answered. She seemed eager to help him, though, so he let her. She did work around the house and then began following him out into the fields. During the third week, he decided to teach her how to drive the mower, and then about a week later the tractor, and finally a couple weeks after that the combine. Despite the fact that her legs barely reached the pedals, she took to it all quite easily and was surprisingly strong.

By Thanksgiving, the corn had been harvested, and the field was bare. Noah stood looking over it at dusk, and he considered the strange luck he'd had in finding this girl. Without her, he might not have finished in time, and his yield—and profit—would have been much less, barely enough to repay loans and keep the power on, not to mention to pay all the medical bills left over from his wife's and daughter's illnesses.

He took the girl to Thanksgiving dinner at Zeke's house. She wore one of his daughter's old dresses, and at the sight of her walking down the staircase before they left, his eyes watered. Over the past few weeks, he found himself crying at strange moments. Sometimes, too, he'd walk into a room and not know what he had come for, or worse, where he was. There was one time he looked in the mirror and didn't even recognize his own face, and then more than once he looked at the girl and really believed she was his daughter. In fact, that's what he thought when he first saw her walking down the stairs, and then when he realized she wasn't, he started crying.

The girl walked up to him and looked into his face. Standing on her tiptoes, she reached up to wipe away his tears. The gesture made him want to cry more, but he swallowed hard and took a deep breath, not wanting to arrive at his brother's looking like he'd been weeping. Zeke and Nancy already worried too much.

With their own parents long gone, and no other family in the area, Thanksgiving dinner was not a big one: Noah and the girl, Zeke, Nancy, and their three kids. Nancy had roasted one of their turkeys and made almost everything else out of their homegrown food. Before they ate, they held hands and said Grace. Only Noah and the girl did not join in.

Noah was hungry and looking forward to his first big home-cooked dinner in months, but when he began to eat, pain ripped through his abdomen as though he'd been shot. He winced and ran to the bathroom. When he threw up, there was blood. He flushed and cleaned off the toilet seat. When he returned to the table, he was no longer hungry, just tired.

"Everything okay?" Zeke asked.

Noah nodded. Nancy asked him if he needed to lie down, and he told her he was fine, he just wanted everyone to enjoy their dinner. In a moment everyone resumed eating and talking, but all through the rest of the meal he could feel the girl's eyes on him, her young forehead wrinkled with worry.

❧

Noah's condition worsened over the next few weeks. He was unable to keep food down, and his bones ached to the point where it was a struggle to get out of bed in the morning. Though he wasn't eating, his abdomen began to swell, looking almost as big as the bellies of the women in the girl's pictures. He had sweats at night and was cold in the day, even sitting by the fire. He watched the girl going about tasks that he would have done, like cooking and cleaning and feeding the chickens. He wondered what would happen to her if—when—he died, and he decided he had to find out who she was and where she had come from. So one day, after weeks of being shut in the house, he suggested they go to the library.

The girl surprised him by repeating the word. Library, she said, like a younger child would, with *berry* at the end. She rolled the word in her mouth as if she had never heard it. It made him wonder if there could have been some truth to his brother's story about the human milk farm, if that's where this girl had come from.

At the library, he sat down at a computer and let the girl wander the stacks. It had been years since he had used the internet, but he went to the one search engine he knew and typed in a few words. *Human milk factory* resulted in a few hits about factory dairy farms. *Women milked* resulted in a few pornographic sites that he quickly closed. Finally, he tried *breastmilk serum*. The first thing he found was a company called Fountain of Youth, which sold an antiaging serum that included human breast milk as an ingredient. So the story wasn't entirely bullshit, after all. On the company's website, however, and in all the news articles mentioning the serum, it was noted again and again that the breast milk in the serum was created in a lab to be an exact replica of human breast milk, and none of it came from real women. Noah looked at the price. One ounce of the serum was over five hundred dollars.

Next he clicked on a few blog posts that echoed the story his brother had told: women kidnapped, mostly immigrant women or women from inner cities and poor rural areas, serving as human milk makers for an expensive serum that promised to reverse aging and protect people from cancer. And not only were women kidnapped and forcibly milked, but they were also forcibly impregnated in order to keep their milk production going. According to one blog, male babies that resulted from these pregnancies were killed upon birth, while female children—at least in the first few years of the project—were kept alive to use as milk makers once their bodies reached maturity. Eventually, though, the corporation decided to discontinue this practice, as they found raising a child to maturity was expensive and time-consuming. It was easier to just continue kidnapping immigrants.

Noah wondered what happened to the young girls born in those first few years. The article did not say. Would they have been killed, too, once the corporation decided they were of no use? Perhaps not. It was one thing to kill a newly born baby, and quite another to kill a toddler. By the date of the post, the girl was just old enough to have been one of these children.

He clicked out of the website and got up to look for the girl.

He could not find her. He looked in the stacks of children's books, and she was not there. He looked by the DVDs, and she was not there. He asked the librarian if she had seen a little girl, about ten years old, dark eyes and hair. The librarian asked her name. Noah stammered a response, trying to explain that she was not his child. The librarian looked at him suspiciously, so he apologized and walked away while the librarian called after him, "Sir? Sir?"

He walked down into the basement and found the girl there, playing with the puppets from the library's storytime shows. He sighed and took her by the shoulders.

"You scared me to death," he said.

She cocked her head. "Dead?" She reached out and held his wrist, as if she were feeling his pulse. "No," she said. "Still here."

⁂

Winter came, and with it a wracking cough that Noah could not shake. The girl watched as he coughed blood into tissues, and she brought him soup and water and blankets. She helped him walk to the bathroom. She herself still bathroomed outside, even in the cold. He was too tired to teach her how to use the toilet. Even with his own daughter, he had let his wife do the dirty work of potty training.

Noah no longer knew the date, but he could tell it was close to Christmas from the cars driving by on the highway with trees strapped to their roofs. Zeke had stopped by the previous week to ask after his health. Noah tried to assure his brother he was fine, but Zeke looked doubtful. When he went to the kitchen to get Noah a drink, the girl was in there doing the dishes. Zeke questioned her, asking if Noah was eating, sleeping, getting around okay. From the other room, Noah could hear his brother's lowered voice growing louder and more frustrated when the girl would not speak. He wondered again what would happen to her when he was gone.

"I'll check on you next week, okay?" Zeke had said before he left. "You really should see a doctor."

As the days passed and he got sicker, Noah began to feel a primal fear rise from his core. He thought he had accepted the inevitability of his death, but there was something in him that resisted it. He did not want to see a doctor, but he also did not want to cease to exist. He couldn't bear the thought that he would not live to see another spring, another crop of corn. The thought that the seasons would keep going and he would not be there to see them was unimaginable.

He remembered something his daughter had said when she was very young, maybe four years old, just beginning to understand life and death: Days aren't going to end, right, Daddy? she'd asked, fear in her eyes. No, he'd reassured her. They just keep going.

One night, he woke in a fever. He had shit the bed. He called out to the girl, still not knowing her name, simply crying, "Girl! Help!"

She ran in, wearing his daughter's pajamas. She did not balk at the smell. She simply lifted him up—he was that light now—and helped him to the bathroom. He was able to make his own bath while she cleaned the bed. She then helped him back into bed and stood over him as he moaned. She seemed to be thinking.

"Up," she said. "Go."

He did not have the energy to resist. If she brought him to a hospital, so be it. At least they would give him medicine for the pain and he could die in peace.

When they got outside, he barely felt the cold. They hobbled to the truck, and she put him in the passenger seat.

"Are you sure?" he asked.

She nodded, her face set and serious. She looked like his daughter did when she was drawing a picture. Such concentration a sort of love. That was something he'd miss.

The girl moved the seat up as far as it could go, started the engine, put her foot on the brake, and then shifted to drive. She was tentative at first, jerking the truck down the road, but eventually she settled into a smooth crawl. It was well after midnight, small snowflakes floating through the air. Each one felt precious. There were no other cars on the road. They passed a house every few miles, mostly dark, some with trees glowing in their windows.

A few miles up the road, close to where he had originally found the girl, she pulled the truck over. She got out, and then walked over to the passenger side and opened his door.

"Where are we?" he asked.

"Home," she said.

⁂

Noah wasn't sure how long they walked in the forest. Half a mile? Three miles? Time was strange now. He leaned on the girl for support.

Deep in the woods, a smell hit him. Even in his present state he could tell what it was. Rotting flesh. The girl walked faster, averting her eyes from what looked like a large pit in the ground. As they kept walking, the smell abated, though it lingered in Noah's nostrils like smoke. Eventually they found a path that led to a dirt road.

Something shined through the dark. A chain-link fence topped with razor wire.

There was a small opening at the bottom of the fence. The girl slid under it.

"Where are you going?" he called.

She reached through the fence to touch his hand.

"Come," she said.

He looked at the buildings inside the fence. There were several barracks and some barns and sheds. It was hard to tell in the dark, but the whole compound looked huge, like it could house thousands of animals. Or women.

He crawled under the fence after the girl, his whole body one ache.

The ground was red dust. The first barracks they passed was brown and shuttered. He and the girl walked past at least a dozen more, silent and dark, until she slipped inside one of them. When he entered, he was hit with a new smell: urine, musk, sweat, and something sweeter. Human milk.

He heard a cry. "Tasha! Tasha!"

Tasha, he thought. He was glad to have a name for her, even here, at the end.

The girl rushed toward the voice, and Noah followed, steadying himself on the edges of the metal cots that lined the room. Before he could reach the spot where the girl had stopped, he had a coughing fit that went on for so long he almost passed out. The girl and the woman she embraced both turned to look at him.

"No," the girl said. She ran to Noah and grabbed his arm, letting him lean on her.

"Tasha," the woman whispered. "Who is he?"

The girl took Noah's arm and rested it on the woman's lap, wrapping the woman's fingers around his wrist. His blood, so slow in his veins. He wondered if she could even feel it. In the lightless room he gazed at her face, her dark eyes, her abundance of dark hair. She looked alarmed. And tender. Her fingers soft on the loose skin of his wrist. Her skin so young, smooth. Her belly so big under her nightgown. Her breasts, already leaking.

"Mama," the girl said. And she lowered Noah's head to her mother's breast. The woman hesitated, looking at her daughter.

"Please," the girl said.

The woman slid the nightgown off her shoulder and slid her nipple into Noah's mouth. So strange, to be a suckling child again, and yet so natural, to fall back into this primary position, the mouth knowing how to move, the throat knowing how to swallow. The girl rested her hand on his shoulder.

His eyes were almost closed, but he could see out of the corner of his vision the other women starting to take notice and sit up—one head after another of long dark hair rising from thin pillows, their nightgowns shining like candles, their bodies swollen with milk or with child, all of them silent, staring not at Noah but at the girl, who stood sentinel beside him and seemed to grow larger in the dark. She was no longer the echo of his daughter, no—more like his mother, giving him life when he had done nothing, really, to deserve it. He wanted in this moment so desperately to do something to deserve it, to at least express his gratitude, but with his mouth full he couldn't form words, and then the women all rose from their beds and came closer, cooing, cocooning their arms around him and the girl, and in this enclosure he felt himself transforming: infant, child, man, larva, pupa, something else entirely.

ONCE BOUND FOR EARTH

JANET IS LESS THAN a mile from the bus yard when she hears it: a faint tap-tap-tapping on the windshield. It looks like hail but grayer, as if a dump truck were kicking back gravel from the road in front of her. Only there is no truck. Besides her bus, there are a couple old pick-ups, but fewer cars on the road than usual, even at this early hour. As she does every morning, Janet left her house at five-thirty to drive her sputtering wood-paneled station wagon to the bus depot so she could get the bus out of the yard before six, so she won't have to rush, so she can drive as slowly and carefully as she wants through the early morning twilight and still get the students to school on time. Some of the other drivers call her crazy, but she knows the students depend on her. And she depends on the job.

She pulls into the parking lot of a diner shaped like a train car. Despite the sign boasting "Quaintest Diner in New Jersey," it's never very busy. When Janet was a kid, she came here with her father for breakfast every Saturday, him smoking the cigarettes that would kill him at forty. They no longer allow smoking in the diner, but every morning when Janet walks in she can still smell the smoke penetrating the scent of bacon grease and burnt toast.

She sits at the counter, orders her coffee to go. The waitress is new and frowns at her. It doesn't bother Janet; she's always been told her natural look is one of bitchiness too. But maybe that's a privilege one gains being a woman over fifty, to stop smiling, stop pretending. She picks up two packets of Sweet'n Low and glances at the TV. Election news. Last night, another Reality-Show President had been elected. Despite a brief stretch of sanity after the first one, they just kept coming, and people kept voting for them. This is the third, almost a carbon copy of the first Conman-in-Chief. Janet wishes now that she had gone to the polls and voted against him, but Janet never voted, never saw the point.

The waitress comes with the coffee. Janet dumps in the Sweet'n Low and takes a sip while she watches the election news shift to local weather. The meteorologist, too cheery, is talking about the strange, sudden hailstorm affecting the Northeast, spanning from D.C. to Boston. Janet looks out the window. Shit. She hates driving in bad weather normally. And from the looks of it, there's nothing normal about this.

In the booth behind her, two old men are talking loudly. One of them says the hail is a sign. The other man is incredulous. The first presses on: You know why libs hate our president so much? The other man starts to reply but is cut off by the first. Cuz he's the second coming, the first man says. The other man chortles. Don't laugh, the first man says. The end times are here! Just look around! He gestures to the stones hitting the window. It ain't climate change, it's God!

Janet shakes her head, gets up off her stool.

"Why don't you shut up, you damn fool," she growls as she walks by their booth. Back in the bus, she checks her phone. No message from the bus company, which means school is still on. Strange. Janet looks down and realizes her hands are shaking.

She shifts into drive and gets back on the road.

ᘚ

Janet's district, in rural northwestern New Jersey, is a microcosm of the country: so much wealth, so much poverty. Janet sees it all. Closest to the school and last to be picked up in the morning are the various iterations of middle-class kids, who live in Cape Cods with their overanxious puppies and younger siblings and IKEA furniture. A few miles up the highway, past cornfields in the middle of Janet's route, is a cluster of cul-de-sacs where the wealthy students live, with their manicured lawns and their mothers hovering in doorways in bedazzled velour sweatsuits. But Janet always starts her morning route at the river, the houses situated along its edge like jagged brown teeth. This is where Janet has lived most of her life and where she raised her son.

Her first stop is always to pick up her favorite student, Leaf, his name like the foliage turning red and brown and falling off the trees all around his tiny clapboard house, which she pulls up to now. There's something about him that reminds her of her own son, when he was around ten years old. So long ago.

の

Janet had her son at nineteen. Dropped out of community college after one semester. Spent her days trying to nurse him but he refused her nipple like he was too good for it. So she gave up and mixed the powdered formula with water, shook the bottle angrily before she picked him up again, and then he drank like a champ, gulped down each bottle and wanted more. He always wanted more. As a kid, more candy. He'd writhe on the floor in the supermarket checkout line while she put back the laundry soap or toilet paper or pads, just to buy him that goddamned king-size Snickers bar. As a preteen, he wanted more clothes and shoes and CDs and things she couldn't afford to give him as a single mother just starting part time as a sub for the bus company. And then as a teen....well. She could've guessed where it was going. When she got home from work, he was up in his room with the door closed and the music blasting. Sometimes he had friends up there, sometimes not. She ignored the smell of pot, or pretended it just was cigarettes, which wasn't too hard because she was still smoking herself at the time.

Sometimes, in the middle of the night when she got up to piss, she walked down the hall to the doorway of his bedroom. The door was always closed. It was quiet in there, finally, at 3 a.m. She wanted to walk in, watch him sleep, try to see her baby in his pockmarked face, but she never did. She never even knew if he was really in there. He might have been out somewhere else, some field or forest or friend's house. She knew there was nothing she could do, so she just went back to sleep, and got up again to shepherd other people's kids to school.

❧

Leaf is nowhere to be seen. Just his nut-brown house, the hail slapping the already-damaged shingles. His skateboard sits alone in the middle of the yard. He's often late. No car in the driveway, but that's not unusual, either. His mother, his only parent, is never there in the mornings, or in the afternoons when Janet drops him off. Working, or drinking, or maybe both. Janet doesn't judge. She knows people, especially mothers, are never just one thing. Still, she often feels sorry for Leaf, so she gives him those few extra minutes to pull himself out of bed, those few extra minutes she doesn't afford the other kids.

But it's been almost ten minutes and Leaf still hasn't emerged, and the hail is coming down harder. Janet checks her phone to see if there are any messages from the school, and then she heads on to the next house. The next two kids are there, a girl and a boy, waiting without umbrellas, coats pulled up over their heads. Janet lets them in and they trudge to the back of the bus. These, too, are kids with absent parents, parents who either work night shift at the factories over in PA or drink all night and are sleeping hard by the time Janet pulls up.

Strangely, after these two, the rest of the river kids are missing until the very last house. Here, Colter lives with his overprotective mother. She's wrapped in a bathrobe, huddled close to her son, holding an umbrella over his head. She walks with him to the bus, but instead of kissing him goodbye, she follows him onto the bus and sits in the seat diagonal to Janet.

"School still on?" she asks.

"Far as I know." Janet wonders if maybe she has missed a message from the school, but there's nothing on her phone.

"They're saying this could be some kind of meteor shower," Colter's mother says.

Janet raises her eyebrows, studies the gray hail hitting her windshield. She thinks she sees a crack starting to form in the corner.

"It's weird, right?" the woman continues. "I'm scared to stay home. Power's out."

Janet begins to understand what she's asking. She wants to ride along. Janet frowns. She's not allowed to have passengers other than the kids, and she's never been written up in her nearly thirty years with the bus company. She looks over at the woman's house, small and dark and probably cold. She looks back at the woman, her tiny son and his crooked glasses.

"Fine," Janet says. She's gotta get going.

Janet drives on, but a feeling begins to form deep in her gut, a stone that turns and gathers hardness until her body is tense, concrete. She drives past the cornfields, into the cul-de-sac. No one is waiting. She continues with only three students, plus the mother. Stop after stop absent of children, the large houses dark, the hail hitting them just as hard as it hits the river houses, but these are roofs with fifty-year shingles, these are houses that can withstand a storm.

Janet squints past the crack beginning to form in the windshield as she makes it into town. Here she finds a few kids waiting, so by the time they get close to school she has ten kids in the bus, a quarter of what she'd normally have. The kids are talking excitedly, sharing theories about what's going on with the weather.

And then, as they drive down the long road to the school, their phones all begin to go off. Chimes, buzzes, beeps, loud alerts Janet has heard before during storms, but never this urgent, never all at once. Janet pulls over. There's a weather alert and a message from the school. The alert is vague. Hazardous weather in the Northeast, from DC to Boston. Take shelter. The school's message is more direct. School closed until further notice. "School closed" is clear enough, but why "until further notice"?

"All right," Janet says, making a halfhearted attempt to sound cheerful but unable to lose the edge in her voice. "We're heading back."

Cheers, high fives. Kids happy to have a day off. But still, there's the rock in Janet's gut. Turning like a planet. Gathering other rocks in its orbit.

※

Janet drives back into town, begins dropping kids off at home. By the third kid, though, she begins to have doubts. What's she dropping them off back to? Are their parents even home? Not her kid, she has to keep reminding herself. Not her job. Just drive.

But then she hears the laughing and cheering die down. It's silent in the back of the bus, too silent for half a dozen kids.

"What's going on back there?" she calls.

At first no one answers. Then one of the older girls walks forward, sits directly behind Janet, and begins speaking in low tones to Colter's mother.

"What is it?" Janet asks.

The girl tells her. She just saw someone online saying this is not a hailstorm or a meteor shower. It's fallout. Apparently Iran or China or North Korea wasn't happy with the election results, and they detonated a bomb somewhere near DC. The administration is trying to hide it, but the fallout's affecting the entire Northeast.

Janet shakes her head. "Bullshit." Normally she doesn't curse around students, but she can't help herself.

"Lots of places are saying it," the girl replies, defensive. "It's all over Twitter. My dad just texted me. When you drop me off, we're driving as far north as we can to get out of range."

Janet stops at a red light, turns around to look at the girl. So young, barely fourteen. Her eyes, large and brown and watery like a dog's, betray a fear that Janet hasn't seen in a child's eyes in a long time. Janet turns back around and speeds up to fifty. She usually never exceeds the speed limit, but now is not the time to worry about being pulled over. There are bigger things to worry about.

When they get to the girl's stop, her parents are waiting on the porch with bags packed, supplies strapped to the top of their minivan, their dog barking, preschool kid brother staring at a tablet. Her father runs up and pops his head in the bus doors. He's breathless.

"Have you heard?"

"Your daughter just told me."

The man furrows his brow, seems to resent her disinterest. "Look, I'm not some kind of conspiracy nut. If I were you, I'd drive north, and don't stop until this stops."

Before Janet can respond, the girl shoves her dad out of the way and gets off the bus, and Janet pushes the button to close the doors. As she pulls away, she watches them in her rearview. A family, embracing like it's the end of the world.

❧

Janet finishes dropping off the rest of the town kids. They're quiet as they exit the bus, no more cheering, no more laughter. Many of them have families waiting for them on porches, worried looks plastered on their faces. Janet speeds past the cul-de-sac, no one to drop off there. Where were those families? In underground bunkers? Did they have some kind of insider knowledge that allowed them to flee before everyone else?

Janet stops at Colter's house, waits for Colter and his mother to exit. They make no move. Janet turns to her, sees the woman staring into her phone, scrolling. She clears her throat, and the woman looks up. The stones pelting the top of the bus are loud now, louder than before. Janet has to raise her voice.

"Your stop."

The woman shakes her head. "We gotta go north."

Janet sighs. "Look, I just drive kids to school. Back and forth. I'm done for the day."

The woman's eyes begin to water, and Colter comes and sits on his mother's lap. She pleads with Janet.

"My car's busted. We don't have a way out."

"It's not even my bus." Janet feels her voice faltering, feels like she's losing this fight, like when she used to try to get her son to eat his peas at dinner. "I could get fired."

The woman slowly stands up, holds her son's hand, and Janet opens the doors. They descend into the weather. Janet thinks about

what Colter and his mother will do, their house cold and dark, no
way out. Her own house dark too, and empty. Her station wagon is
big enough, maybe, to squeeze them all in, but it's a beater, and not
equipped to make a trip of more than a few miles. If she takes the
bus, will she get fired? Maybe. Definitely. But does it even matter
anymore? Janet isn't sure. Colter and his mother are halfway through
their front yard when Janet opens the doors again.

"Come on," she shouts. "I'll get us out of here. But there's one
thing I gotta do first."

❦

She drives back toward the river. Springsteen's song pops into
her head, something about going down to a river and diving in. Her
life, she thinks, has been kind of like a Springsteen song. Her life, all
of it culminating here: no family of her own to shelter with, just this
worried woman, her son, and these two other river children, the boy
and the girl who didn't want to be dropped off to their empty houses.
And one other kid she knows she must find.

When she gets to Leaf's house, she sees it's dark. She tells her
passengers to stay put and wait for her. She opens the door and exits, pulling her jacket over her head, but the falling stones still hurt,
sting, cold little insect bites. She runs up to the doorway and knocks.
No answer. She peers in the window. Blackness. She tries the door-
knob. It's open. Course it is. People here don't lock their doors, partly
because they've never been taught to do so, partly because the locks
are broken, but mostly because they know they have nothing worth
stealing.

She steps in. It smells like cigarettes and cats. She steps over a
plastic takeout container. She calls Leaf's name. Nothing.

She hears some noise from the kitchen and walks toward it. A white cat with pink eyes is eating out of a pot scabbed in oatmeal. The cat hisses at her, and she jumps. She steps out the back door and sees a fat beagle tied to a chain, whimpering. She walks over to him but stops short when he growls, a low, deep growl. Janet kneels down.

"It's okay." She holds out her hands. The hail smacks against her palms like tiny bullets.

She reaches into her pocket and finds a mint that had been there for months.

"Here, boy," she says, holding it out.

The dog creeps forward and sniffs, then licks the candy, then takes the whole thing into its mouth and chews. The cracks and pops sound like he's crunching through bone. She smooths her hand over its fur, wet and cold and soft. It has been so long since she has run her hand along the back of any animal. She unhooks him, and he follows her back to the bus.

Janet can think of only one place lost boys go when they want to run away.

⁂

When Janet's son was a teenager, he was never home. To be fair, neither was she. He always said he was at a friend's, or playing basketball at the school's blacktop, but one day she found out where he really was. On one of the back roads there was an underpass, graffitied with decades of names and tags and teenage loves. He hadn't come home all night, so she went out looking for him, walking the streets, calling his name like he was a lost dog. Finally, she found him at the underpass. He wasn't conscious. There were needles and broken bottles littered around his body, along with a single, blackened silver spoon. And he was alone. The smell of cigarette smoke lingered in the air, as if someone, or a group of someones, had just left, left her son there to die. She carried his body all the way home to call 911; she didn't have a cell phone then, and though she searched his pockets frantically, she couldn't find his, either. Halfway home, she couldn't hold his weight anymore, so she had to drag him, holding him under the armpits, his legs scraping the gravel, one of his shoes falling off during the journey. He had scrapes all down the length of his legs. But he didn't die. Not then.

❧

Since that night, Janet has tried to avoid the underpass, easy enough since the clearance is too low for the bus, anyway. There was one recent night she drove by it without meaning to, and she saw in the glow of the orange streetlamp two figures, a young man kissing a young woman deeply on the mouth, pressing her up against the side of the underpass. They were probably high, she thought, but still she felt a sense of bitterness fading to envy and loss, for herself or for her son she wasn't sure. In any case, she knows this is the kind of place kids without parents go. Kids who want, ironically, someplace safe. Like a cave. Something to cradle them, shelter them.

She approaches the underpass and pulls the bus over on the side of the road. From the back, the two river kids ask why they're stopping, and Colter's mother groans. "We don't have much time," she says, scrolling through her phone. "Please hurry." She hugs her son tightly on her lap.

Janet exits the bus. The dog begins to follow her, pokes its nose out of the door, but then turns around and climbs back in. The hail, or whatever it is, is coming down hard, gray all around. She can barely see anything, but as she walks up to the lip of the underpass, in the dark she sees a figure, slight, lithe. Leaf.

She calls his name.

He steps forward hesitantly. He has brown eyes, so big, too big for his skinny face. He already looks aged, like a worn-out old man, has probably looked that way since kindergarten, probably will forever. However long forever is for him.

"I was supposed to meet some friends here," he says. Like an apology.

Janet shakes her head. "Everyone's leaving." She has to shout to be heard over the slapping hail.

"What's going on, Miss Janet?" He always calls her Miss, even when she tells him not to. His voice holds the husky beginnings of puberty.

"I don't know," she calls. "But we're getting out of here. Where's your mom?"

Leaf retreats to the underpass, stares out at her, only the whites of his eyes visible. "I don't know," he says, his voice echoing. "She never came home last night."

Janet knows what she must do, but also knows not to command. Just to ask.

"Do you want to come with us?" He doesn't answer at first, and she's not sure he's heard. She asks again.

Finally he calls, "Where?"

"North," she says. "Somewhere safe."

❧

The summer after his first overdose, Janet sent her son to her aunt's farm at the tip of Maine, near the Canadian border. Her aunt never married, was a tough, strong woman who lived what seemed a wholesome and monastic life, growing her own food, taking care of horses, teaching Home Ec part time at the local high school. She lived a hard life, but it was the good kind of hard, different than down here in Jersey. A clean life. That's what she sent her son up there for. To get clean. And he went.

The house was big and white with chipped paint, a large porch, a bright kitchen, and wood floors that dated back centuries. Janet almost wanted to stay there herself, but had to get back to work bussing the rich kids to summer camps, and she knew her son would be better off without her. He spent the summer, from what she gathered in his letters, riding horses and taking care of them, baling hay, planting and harvesting crops, and when he returned in the fall, he looked like a man: filled out, with the beginnings of a beard, tan and bright-eyed. Happy. And then, three weeks later, on his seventeenth birthday, she found him dead on the toilet with a needle in his arm. Very common, the paramedics said.

Nothing is common about a child's death, though. Every time it is a new bomb, a new form of destruction, a new grief, each one unique like a fingerprint. When addicts stop using, they told her, and then start up again, they tend to use at the same amount they used before, but their bodies can't handle it because they'd been clean, almost like first-time users. So, it was her fault. By getting him clean, she had sentenced him to death.

After that, she hadn't talked to her aunt. She hadn't even informed her of her son's death, though the old woman found out somehow, because she was at the funeral. She was Janet's only remaining relative, but Janet stopped all contact with her. Stopped all contact with everyone. Some days the only people she speaks to are these kids. In a way, these kids, even the snotty ones, have become her only family. Fifteen years now. She doesn't even know if her aunt is still alive, if the farmhouse is still standing. But it's the only safe place she can think of.

⌘

The northbound highway is clogged. People honk, scream, as if somehow that will make the line move. The drive to the farmhouse should take less than twelve hours, but by dusk they are still only halfway there, a roadside stop somewhere on the border of Massachusetts and New Hampshire. Janet waits at the pump, refueling the bus, while Colter's mom takes the kids to get something to eat inside at the McDonald's. Janet shakes her head. Even at the world's end those golden arches will still be standing.

She drives all night, taking gulps of coffee when she finds herself nodding off. By now, the windshield is so cracked she can barely see out of it, but she continues on, the four children all sleeping in their seats near the front of the bus. Even Colter's mother is sleeping, her phone dead from endless scrolling, her last update to Janet something contradictory. Seems left-leaning outlets claim this is a nuclear attack in direct relation to the recent election, while fringe religious sites assert this is a heaven-sent hail of meteorites, a sign of the end times. Most major news outlets, though, are insisting it is nothing more than a strange hailstorm brought on by climate change, not all that different from other strange storms they've seen in the last few years. This is supposed to be a comforting option.

Outside, the cold bare ground, the yellow grass, the fields, are covered with small stones that shine like coins as dawn approaches. The bare trees don't acknowledge that anything has changed. The birds begin to chirp again.

※

Just after dawn, Janet turns onto the long gravel drive toward the farmhouse. When she stops the bus, it is silent. No more pings, no more clangs, no more knocks on the roof. The hail, or whatever it was, has stopped falling. She looks back, and everyone is still sleeping. Only the dog wakes, stretches, lumbers toward her. She reaches to stroke its head. She hasn't had a pet since her son died. Gave away their dog a few weeks after he passed. Couldn't bear to be close with something whose life was so fragile.

She opens the door and walks out into the crisp air. The dog follows, stopping to lift its leg against the bus tire. She realizes she doesn't know what she will say, if her aunt even lives here anymore. If it is a stranger who opens the door, it might feel less strange. It looks like the house is abandoned, and it's so quiet it feels like the whole world is abandoned, like this is the end of the line. She hears a noise and turns around. It is the nickering of a horse, shiny and black. She walks up to the fence. The horse approaches her, and she smooths her hand along its nose, closes her eyes.

When she opens them, she sees a figure in a white nightgown approaching. In the misty dawn, it looks like a ghost and Janet has a moment of fear and unreality, but as the woman approaches, Janet recognizes her—it is her aunt, hobbling in bare blue-veined feet to greet her.

Her aunt opens her mouth, but no sound comes out. Janet too. The old woman is breathless by the time she reaches Janet. She leans on the fence.

"This was his favorite horse," she says after a long silence. "When he was here. This horse, it came in all skinny and malnourished and aggressive, but your son helped bring it back to life." Her fingertips trace its muzzle. "That's something I always hoped to tell you. I'm glad I get to."

Janet closes her eyes again. In the darkness behind her eyelids she hears the bus doors open, hears the sounds of sneakers squeaking against the steps like a flock of tiny birds, hears the voices of Leaf and the other three children approaching and imagines the kids merging into one line behind her, all of them waiting at the gate to some many-roomed house where they will be taken care of, where nobody will be left behind.

She opens her eyes and for a moment she thinks she sees him in the group of children, her son, Jonathan, hale and happy and young, but then he is gone. It is enough, maybe, to be here for just a short while. It is enough that she tried.

CHILDREN AND OTHER
ARTIFACTS

BEFORE URSULA AND HUNTER married, they agreed they would not bring children into the world. Too many wars, he'd said. Too much poverty, she'd said. Too many car accidents and stupid television shows and violent video games and expensive sneakers and nuclear weapons. Too much sadness. Too much selfishness. Too much technology. Besides, the polar ice caps were melting. Besides, children born in the twenty-first century came out of the womb already spoiled, already bad.

But after they'd been married five years, whenever Ursula saw the moon-round bellies of women in pregnancy magazines or watched a neighbor stroll her child down the sidewalk at dusk in a frilly pink-and-white baby carriage, she felt some primal need snake its way from her womb to her stomach to her throat, until one day it came out her mouth. She begged her husband for a child. Each time she asked he said no, no, until a year later, finally, he agreed, but on one condition: that their baby be born as if it were from another time period. It didn't matter which era—just not the twenty-first century or the second half of the twentieth. He laughed when he said it, but Ursula was so ecstatic she began picking names—Delilah, Selah, Micah. All the names she picked ended with a sigh, the sound of wistfulness, or disappointment, or desire. She readied the nursery.

❧

The baby dropped out of Ursula's body like a bomb, and afterward she was so spent she didn't look to see if the child was a boy or a girl. In fact, what she'd birthed was technically neither. The baby was a miniature WWII soldier, equipped with damp green uniform and helmet slick with mucous, translucent nails and tiny hands gripped around the butt of a semi-automatic rifle.

When Ursula finally woke and saw her child, she mumbled to her dumbstruck husband that the rifle was an M1 Garand. She knew this because her grandfather, who'd been an American soldier in WWII, had a collection of rifles he used to show her while telling stories of the war. The only stories she remembered revealed none of the violence or horrors: her grandfather traveling on foot through French forests, getting lost, using moss as a compass to guide him north; her grandfather in the bustling German streets on the day of a solar eclipse, picking up a piece of green glass, giving it to a pretty girl to look through as the streets darkened.

Despite the doctors' bewilderment, they declared the infant healthy, and Ursula was happy with her new soldier-baby, whom she named Johnny. The child wailed whenever Ursula tried to dress him in anything but the fatigues he was born in, so every week she would have to take the fatigues out just a little bit, lengthen the legs and arms as the baby grew. It was difficult to stick thread through the eye of a needle when her eyelids were half-closed with exhaustion, but Ursula did it happily, because she loved her son.

Hunter wasn't sure if he did. He thought about it a lot, considered if he loved Johnny as he burped him, as he watched him sleep, as he changed his diaper. He thought about it on the long drive to work and then at his desk at the post office where he sorted mail—mostly bills and advertisements, not many real handwritten letters left anymore—which he then delivered to houses three times the size of the one he shared with his wife. On the drive home he thought about his son some more, weighing the pros and cons. The more he thought about it, the less sure he became that he loved his child.

As Johnny grew, Hunter became more and more sure that, in fact, he *didn't* love the baby. Johnny liked to play only with toy boats and tanks and planes and parachute men. When Hunter sat Johnny beside him on the couch and began to read him *Where the Wild Things Are* or *The Velveteen Rabbit*, the boy smacked away the book and reached for his toy grenade, which he then launched at his father. Johnny didn't enjoy other things Hunter used to enjoy when he was a kid, like drawing or coloring or making music by banging pots and pans. In fact, Johnny startled easily at the makeshift music of pots and pans and even at the Beethoven records Hunter tried to play for him. But, though shaken, Johnny didn't cry; he was stoic, and he rushed at the record player with his gun, unloaded of course. Johnny cried when the gun wasn't by his side, like other children cried when their favorite teddy bears were taken away. Hunter wasn't sure he should be allowed to have the gun, suggested they replace it with a toy gun while the kid was asleep, but Ursula insisted he keep it because it was the only thing that soothed him when he was upset.

One night, after Ursula put Johnny down to sleep in his bed—or *barracks*, as the toddler called it in his babble-speak—Hunter approached her as she was lengthening their son's pants yet again, in the quiet lamplit corner of the nursery surrounded by unused picture books, and told her that he was unhappy with how their son was turning out.

"I'm sorry," she said, looking up from her sewing. "Why?"

"He's too…modern, or something," Hunter replied. "He's only interested in tanks and guns. I hoped our kid would at least like to read, so we could have something in common."

Ursula put Johnny's fatigues down on her lap. She knew there was no arguing with her husband when he got like this. He was a stubborn man, stubborn about politics, about culture, about philosophy, about where the utensils were kept in the kitchen, and now, stubborn about babies, too.

"Maybe he'll grow out of it," she ventured.

"He won't."

Ursula put the needle and thread down on the table beside her. As she did so, she accidentally pricked her ring finger and a bead of blood blossomed on the tip. It grew larger, slowly, and dripped on her dress, small sunburst stain hovering over her belly button. She closed her eyes for what she thought was a minute, and when she opened them again her soldier-baby and all the remnants of his existence were gone. Her belly was big once again. She sighed, picked out new names.

❧

Their daughter was born wearing petticoats. And bloomers. And a long silk dress with a bustle. And a plumed hat with a veil which covered the baby's face and which the baby would not let the doctor, nor her father, nor her mother lift even an inch to see her bare skin.

After his initial shock, Hunter rocked the child and smiled; he liked the Victorian era, its writers, its morals, its culture, its architecture. Ursula wasn't so sure. As she held the infant, exhausted from a difficult and painful birth, she missed the smell of baby skin. Nothing, not even the child's feet or hands, was uncovered, so the sweet, damp, familiar smell of baby skin and scalp was nowhere to be found. The wife searched for it, sniffing her daughter all over, but she just smelled like starched linens and cried when her mother's nose burrowed into her neck. Ursula named the baby, with a sigh, Victoria.

Victoria was a fussy child. She cried at the oddest things. Pointing at the bare legs of tables, chairs, and the bench of the old, out-of-tune piano Hunter had rescued from the side of a snowy road, Victoria wailed until her mother or father covered the legs with long tablecloths or sheets. Certain words her parents used set Victoria off, too. For instance, the words *leg* and *arm* caused the child to cry so often that Hunter and Ursula began to unconsciously use the term *limb* instead. Even when they thought Victoria was too young to understand, she cried in a recriminating way whenever her parents argued and used curse words, so Ursula and Hunter's arguments got quieter and quieter until they had to whisper their anger into one another's ears as if they were instead exchanging sweet nothings.

Most often, their arguments were about Victoria. Hunter was sure she had a learning disability, because by the age of two she had not yet started speaking. Instead of speech, Victoria expressed herself by rearranging the flowers in the house, and if there was no particular flower for what she felt, she drew it, creating beautiful pictures that resembled watercolor paintings except they were rendered with waxy, broken crayons. Ursula, who was let go from her job during her first pregnancy, spent all day with Victoria and came to understand her language. Whenever Victoria was told that she couldn't play with her dolls and she had to eat lunch instead, the child plucked the yellow carnations from their vase and laid them, dripping, at her mother's feet. When Victoria fell down as she was toddling around on their back deck, instead of sobbing, she crawled over to the garden and pulled out a marigold. An anemone meant Victoria was sick; a red rose meant she loved her mother. And despite the fact that the baby never did smell like a baby and always turned away from Ursula's breast as if offended at the very sight of it, her mother loved her, too.

While at first Hunter liked his Victorian child, in the end, her language of flowers baffled him. In the dawn twilight before he left for work and in the dusk after he got home, Ursula tried to teach him, but he didn't understand, couldn't believe their daughter was really trying to communicate through floral arrangements.

"It's nonsense," he said one Sunday afternoon. "She needs to learn to speak."

It was summer, and Ursula was kneeling down in the dirt of the garden, planting more flowers where Victoria had plucked up the morning glories.

"I'm just disappointed," he said. "I thought our child would be so much smarter."

Ursula looked at her husband, his face aged and wounded like a bruised peach, his glasses glinting in the sun, his hands paper-cut from handling letters at work, bills at home.

"I thought you didn't like children who talk too much," she said. "I thought you liked the idea of a child who doesn't speak until spoken to."

Hunter threw up his hands. "But I am speaking to her! I'm speaking to her all the time. I tell her I love her, and she doesn't even know how to say *Daddy.*"

"Maybe she doesn't need to learn to speak," Ursula mused, fingering a rose head. "She's still smart. She's still beautiful."

Hunter knelt down, cupped his hand around his Ursula's ear, whispered, "Beautiful? We've never even seen her face, because she always has that fucking veil on!"

Ursula cupped her hands around Hunter's ear and said, "*You* were the one that asked for this, asshole. Remember?"

Hunter looked sadly through the glass door at his daughter arranging flowers at the kitchen table, then looked at his wife. He whispered in her ear again.

"I know, but she's just not *right.*"

Ursula sighed, another sigh in a long marriage of sighs. As she moved to stand up, her finger brushed the thorn of a rose-stem and a cloud passed over the sun, darkening the garden. When the sun reappeared a moment later—an hour, a day, a week later?—the yard was full of blooming flowers, and Ursula was pregnant again. Through the glass doors, there was no sign of Victoria; there was no sign of her anywhere. The only thing she left behind, which Ursula and Hunter later found lying across their pillows, was a single black rose.

꙳

During labor, Ursula thought her doctor was performing an episiotomy, but it was the new baby himself doing the cutting with a long silver sword. He brandished that sword when he was finally out and the mystified midwife held him. The baby was a miniature knight, fully equipped with clanking plate armor and helmet, which the doctor lifted off his head so his mother could see his blinking blue eyes. Hunter, no longer struck speechless as with the last two births, said they should name their son Gawain. Ursula objected, covering her son's tiny ears by gently placing the helmet back over his head, telling her husband that she would not have her son be the butt of jokes, and that, besides, she's the one who's been through labor three times, so she was going to pick the name.

She named him Arthur, Art for short.

At first Hunter was perplexed by Art; he hardly looked like a real boy or even a real human being. Whenever Hunter looked at the child, sleeping peacefully in his crib in a full suit of armor, pinholes in the face plate so he could breathe, Hunter didn't feel like he was looking at his son but rather a slightly larger version of the statue of a knight that he remembered seeing on his father's bureau when he was a kid. That old silver statue was the only thing his father owned that was worth something substantial. He always imagined it a relic, as if the statue had really been passed down from the Middle Ages.

The knight was mysterious, its whole body and face cloistered behind armor, much as his father was hidden from him when Hunter was a child, and as his own son was hidden from him now.

Despite Art's resemblance to the statue, Hunter had fun playing with him as Arthur grew into a toddler. He took his high school fencing pole out of the attic and jousted with the child, not caring that his son always beat him. Whenever Ursula tried to join in, Art never wanted to joust with her; he'd usher her back to the couch, cover her legs with a quilt, and fortify her body with pillows. At those times she felt less his mother than some anonymous woman he was protecting.

Art's attitude toward Ursula revealed itself one night when he toddled into his parents' bedroom, dragging his sword behind him like a security blanket, just as Ursula was crying out under Hunter's thrusts. Art rushed toward the bed, slicing the sword through the air, and attacked his naked father, who yelped in surprise and whose first reaction was to cover his genitals with cupped hands. The toddler repeatedly slashed at his father's thighs. If Ursula hadn't replaced Art's real sword with a plastic sword one night while the he was sleeping, he probably would have killed his father. Luckily, Hunter had only a few scratches from the rough edges of the plastic.

Ursula was amused at how Freudian it all was, thought she'd have loved to tell this story to her college friends, if they had stayed in touch. But Hunter was not amused. He spanked the boy, shut him in his bedroom, then returned to his wife, face red, and huffed, "This kid is going to grow up to be the next Jack the Ripper."

Ursula laughed. "I think you're off by a few hundred years."

"What?"

"Not to mention Jack the Ripper liked to kill women, not chop off his daddy's balls."

Ursula let the sheet drop from her chest, motioning Hunter to come back to bed. He shook his head, pulled on his boxers, said,

"He's way too violent. What if he becomes one of those kids who shoots up his whole school? God knows kids are gonna make fun of him in that armor he refuses to take off."

Hunter paced the length of their small room, his body thin and pale, his shoulders hunched forward. This posture of defeat and helplessness shot pity through Ursula, and then anger.

"We got a kid from a different era," she said. "We didn't get the era itself."

"I just said I wanted a kid that had old-fashioned qualities. What's wrong with that?"

"Nothing," Ursula replied. "But why can't you just be satisfied with what you have?"

Hunter sat on the edge of the bed, slumped forward as if under the weight of invisible armor. "How could anyone be satisfied with anything in this world?"

There was silence in the room, and Ursula sighed, ready for the lamp to flicker beside her, for clouds to cover the summer moon, for a flash of lightning to wake her with a new pregnancy.

"I'm so tired," she said.

Hunter lay down beside her. "I am, too. Why'd we even decide to have kids?"

Ursula turned her back to him, picked up a book from the bedside table and opened it, the sharp corner of a page slicing her finger.

"Maybe we didn't decide," she whispered.

But Hunter was already asleep. When he woke at dawn, Ursula was standing near the window, belly full like the sun.

❧

Their next baby babbled out his mother's birth canal, asking questions in a language no one could understand. He wore a toga, stained by amniotic fluid and tied at the shoulder. Ursula had wanted to name this next child Micah, but in her exhausted delirium that lasted almost a week after they brought the baby home, she neglected to give their son a name. She fell asleep anywhere she could—the couch, the kitchen table, the foyer floor, the top of the running dryer, on tender spring grass amid insect families dying and being born in the cool mud—and she always woke in a pool of her own breast milk. Meanwhile, Hunter brought the infant to the town library, where he tried to translate his son's language.

Turned out, as Hunter had suspected, the baby was speaking Greek. He was elated—they had birthed a philosopher!—and he rushed home, eager to tell Ursula that they should name the baby Socrates. But before he could, his son spoke to him in English, drooling a little out of his toothless mouth, and insisted that his name *must* be Aesop. Hunter thought Aesop was not nearly as good a name as Socrates, nor was he as important an historical figure.

"And is there a reason *you* should pick my name?" the baby asked.

"Because I'm your father."

"And that grants you authority?"

"Well, yes," Hunter replied, his voice sharpening.

"And what is the nature of fatherhood that grants you the authority to name me?"

Hunter made a sharp turn and looked at his son through the rearview mirror, little flashing eyes challenging his father.

The baby continued, "Shouldn't a name belong to the one whose existence it is attached to? Or can names even *belong* to anyone?"

Hunter pulled into their driveway, put the car in park, whipped his head around.

"Babies get their names from their families, okay?"

"And what is the nature of a family and its relationship to the individual that leads you to believe the family should have priority over the individual?"

Hunter exited the car, unbuckled his son from the car seat, picked him up, slammed the door.

"Families have a history of names," he said. "Names are passed down. I think that gives parents some kind of historical authority to name their children."

As he carried the baby up to the porch, the child spit up on his shoulder and then said, "You use history as your reason. But what reason does history have? Is there even such a thing as history? Is your knowledge of time so absolute that you can say without a doubt that there exists such a thing as past, present, or future? "

Hunter paused at the front door, looking down into the doughy, expectant face of his child. There was no use. This week-old baby was more argumentative than anyone Hunter had ever met, including himself, and this fact inspired annoyance more than pride. He carried the child into the house like a loaf of bread, with only enough tenderness to not crush it. He woke Ursula, who was sleeping on the wooden stairs.

"The kid wants to be called Aesop," he told her. "Oh, and he's been speaking Greek, but apparently he can speak English, too."

Ursula sat up and took her son from Hunter's arms. The weight of the baby, despite its tiny size and light clothing, was like a sack of bricks.

"I can't argue with him anymore," Hunter told her, walking away.

Ursula didn't reply. She looked down at her now-silent child. He opened his mouth for her breast, and she smiled, imagining what verbal lashing his soft-gummed yap had given her husband, who was ripe for it. Yes, the gums were soft, but she did not offer the child her breast; she was afraid of letting it attach to her. She was waiting for the moment when some flash or stab would rid the world of this still-unnamed child and replace it with another, when time would circle back, again, to a new first pregnancy. Time kept circling back, but she was getting older and older. She wanted to cry, but only her breasts wept.

⁂

Hunter apologized for getting angry with their child-philosopher and promised Ursula their next baby would last, would be the one they keep forever, but Ursula was nervous throughout her pregnancy. What if this kid didn't work out? What kind of baby would pop out this time, and where would it come from—*when* would it come from? Could she even physically endure another pregnancy?

Ursula and Hunter argued about the baby before it was born. Ursula blamed Hunter for putting this curse on them in the first place. Hunter blamed Ursula, arguing that she must be subconsciously choosing the historical periods from which their children came. Ursula argued that she'd rather not have children at all if they were going to keep getting rid of them, especially after she already loved them. He asked, then—knowing as he did so it was a question both stupid and cruel, but unable to stop himself—how could she love a person that she only knew for a few days, a few weeks, even a few years? Her eyes shone as she said, I loved you after a few days. Silence followed, then, while with faraway eyes they remembered the days of their youth, when her hair was long and light brown like a muddy lake and his jaw was still slim and covered with only the slight fuzz of his late bloom into a man. Ursula said, "You were a rare boy, so shy, so sad, so disappointed with the world." Hunter put his hand on her belly, said, "I swear this is the last time." She said, "I'm doing this to make you happy." He said, "I'm doing this to make *you* happy." And the conversation was the same every day.

Their next baby was a difficult birth, and he tumbled out howling, wearing a loincloth. Ursula wondered if his head had been misshapen in the delivery process, because his forehead was unusually low, his brow ridge stuck out like a shelf, he seemed to have no chin, his nose looked like it had been smashed down the middle with a shovel, and his overbite was pronounced even before he had any teeth, although teeth began to sprout from his bleeding gums much faster than normal. Ursula loved him precisely because of these abnormalities.

Rocking him one day, it occurred to her that throughout her life she tended to love people or things because of their defects or pitiable qualities. For instance, a stuffed animal that she saw at a flea market once when she was a child, a panda bear with a missing eye, its nose skewered to one side, its mouth a lopsided mess, its white parts gray, smelling like dust and mothballs and vomit. A cat that she took in as a teenager, one side of its orange fur torn off, its exposed skin pink, raw, festering with worms. A dog she cared for that lost all its legs in an accident and had to slither around on the floor like a snake until it died. Even her husband, when she met him, a gangly teen too smart for his own good, with glasses too big for his face, sadness too big to be contained in his body, so some of it spilled over around him into a puddle that once in a while looked beautiful, like an oil spill in rain.

They named this child Micah, the breath at the end of his name a long-awaited sigh of relief. He was a quiet kid who liked to eat and sleep, as if he were more animal than human. His body grew much faster than normal; by the time he was one, he was the size of a three-year-old and knew how to run well enough to chase squirrels in the backyard. But he couldn't speak except for grunts and groans, which, like the mute Victoria, frustrated Hunter. He tried to hide his frustration from Ursula, to make good on his promise, and he tried to enjoy playing with twigs and rocks with his son in the yard, because he wanted his wife to be happy.

Micah stayed in their lives longer than any of the other children had, Hunter holding back his reservations about the child out of respect for Ursula, Ursula holding back her worries out of spite and stubbornness. But both worried about him. He'd be entering kindergarten in the fall and hadn't yet learned to speak clearly, much less read. He did know how to draw, and his parents encouraged him in that, trying to remain positive, neither one wanting to say the wrong word that might plunge them into another loss, another pregnancy. Both believed, somehow, their words had caused their previous children to disappear.

But Micah's social skills seemed lacking, too: when they brought him to the park, he pushed other kids off the swings or the slide, yelling at them in gibberish, protecting his territory with a violence that seemed worse than normal childhood behavior. But the most worrisome thing about Micah was the way he often strayed from his parents and put himself in dangerous situations, such as when he chased squirrels up the hill beyond their back yard or trailed big dogs to neighbors' houses, sometimes running into the street so swiftly neither Hunter nor Ursula could grab him until he was already on the other side, poking at the dogs with sticks he'd sharpened with his own nails and teeth.

Eventually they decided they'd put a fence up around the front and back yards, but before they could do it the inevitable happened: one spring day, Micah was struck by a car while running across the street. Ursula and Hunter had been watching him from plastic chairs on the lawn, but neither was fast enough to grab him by the T-shirt before he darted into the road. It didn't matter that he was fifth in a line of children that had disappeared without a trace; Ursula reacted like any mother would, screaming and crying and sprinting to her baby's body, which was twisted and bleeding in the road, still as a fossil. Hunter trailed his wife, overwhelmed with the need to swallow but unable to, unable to breathe for what felt like hours as they waited in the hospital for the pronouncement to be made, and when it was, they felt the sky darken suddenly as their child disappeared. Only this time there was no replacement.

They followed the doctor into the room where Micah was lying in bed, his head bandaged, tubes in his nose attached to a machine that was the only thing keeping him alive, even though the doctor said there was no hope for improvement, there was no brain activity, and there never would be again.

They had almost expected the bed to be empty, almost expected Micah's body to have mysteriously disappeared like the others had. But his body was there, as real as a rock, and they had to make the decision, tell the doctor whether or not to pull the plug. Neither Ursula nor Hunter could speak for nearly ten minutes as the doctor stood beside them, waiting for their decision. Finally, Hunter knew the word he had to say, and he spoke it with the knowledge that he was doing it for his wife, to spare her the pain of saying it.

"Now," he said.

❧

Now, Hunter and Ursula are alone again in a house that seems bigger than before, despite or perhaps because it is still filled with remnants of Micah. They go through the painful task of putting his toys away in boxes, folding his clothes and placing them in wooden chests which they then carry to the attic, out of sight. Ursula and Hunter hold one another closer at night, heads touching so that it seems they're sharing the same dreams. This time, neither blames the other.

It is a long time before they make love, and when they do, it's as quick as a sneeze, out of animal need, on the floor of the tiny apartment they're renting because Hunter quit his job at the post office and their home is being foreclosed. When Ursula comes, her vision goes dark and she sees lightning beneath her eyelids.

In a few weeks she finds she's pregnant. In her first trimester she cries more than she ever has in her life, her tears beading on plastic flowers and wetting the pages of books and making puddles on the linoleum so that when Hunter comes home from interviews in his dress shoes he sometimes slips. He helps Ursula in and out of bed, makes macaroni and cheese dinners for her, reads children's books to her before she goes to sleep to ward off bad dreams. He mothers her in that tender way until the day she goes into labor, a snowy winter morning. They wade through gray slush and speed down slippery roads, car still half-covered with snow. The hospital is new to them, less familiar than the old one, but nevertheless a place with good doctors who will deliver their child.

It's a messy birth, like the messy day. Ursula pushes and pushes but the baby will not come, so the doctor does a cesarean section. Mercifully, the curtain prevents her from seeing the doctor cut her open; she looks only at her husband's hand holding hers. His veins stick out, swollen, the blood running through them not the same as hers but mingled with hers in their child's body, a new life made of their blood. But as the child is being taken out of her belly she wonders if they've really *made* it, if anyone at any time in history truly chose to have a child, if anyone could possibly make a conscious decision to create a new human life, knowing the inevitable ocean that the rivers of their blood lead to.

Meanwhile, Hunter looks at his wife's insides for the first time and wonders at the magic of her messy body, the miracle of that ugly place inside her that has created the existence of the child being lifted out to take a first breath. He grips her hand a little tighter.

And then Hunter and Ursula join gazes upon their baby: a girl, screaming out of her black void of a mouth surrounded by raw, pink, splotchy flesh, an anonymous infant like the millions of other infants born this day, naked and nameless.

A LOVE LETTER FROM
VERY FAR AWAY

THE FIRST OBELISK APPEARED in a cornfield outside our town of Bowling Green, Ohio, just a few years after we'd survived the latest pandemic, right when we thought things were returning to normal. It probably wasn't the right word for the structure, *obelisk*, but that's how the first article referred to it, and the name stuck. It was thirty feet tall, and pretty wide, a sideways trapezoid stuck into the earth by one of its sharp corners. The surface was smooth black like obsidian, though the scientists who tested it said that's not what it was. They ultimately admitted, rather sheepishly, they couldn't tell *what* it was.

It started out as a local wonder. News stations referred to it as an Object of Mysterious Origin, or OMO; alien enthusiasts from neighboring counties came by the dozen and made comparisons to *2001: A Space Odyssey*; parents took their children to gaze and wonder and try to climb the thing with no luck. Our own son was seventeen at the time, teetering on the edge of adulthood, but even we took him once. He stood there, disinterested, staring instead at his phone, and you and I, we simply regarded our reflections in the glassy black of the trapezoid's surface, wondering what would happen to us when he eventually left the nest. What would we have to hold us together?

Soon, structures popped up in other places across the country. First, another cornfield, this one in Iowa. Then a farm in upstate New York. Beside Lake Pontchartrain in Louisiana. On a mountaintop in Colorado. In the middle of the Arizona desert. Right along the border in New Mexico. In an alleyway in Oakland, cracking concrete. And finally, in the Badlands, where no one noticed for a while.

The first obelisk arrived on the spring equinox. By the time we realized they were popping up all over the country, the politicians were rabid. They assumed it was an act of aggression from another country. They speculated that the material might emit some kind of dangerous energy. Local officials roped off the structures with police tape, a large yellow square at least one hundred yards on each side. It reminded me of those years back, when the pandemic hit and the playgrounds were closed off with caution tape as if they were crime scenes. Our son was nine then, at an age where he still sometimes asked to go to the playground but was beginning to prefer video games. When the playgrounds closed, he happily resigned himself to pre-teenagehood, and I, of course, mourned.

While new buds shivered in the wind, politicians argued about who sent the obelisks and why, throwing accusations like cherry bombs. By summer, though, these structures had been spotted in almost every country across the world, dotting the globe like jagged black jewels. Some of those on the far right took a different angle. They were no longer a threat but a gift from God. They argued that America had received more of these blessings than any other country because America was the most blessed country on earth. They urged local officials to remove the yellow tape and encouraged all Christians to flock to the rocks. ("Flock to the Rock" even became a national catchphrase for a while.) Some began setting up camp there, the most devout followers making fervent attempts to chip away at the obelisks, hoping to collect fragments like the relics of saints. The structures, though, could not be broken, not even a sliver. That in itself should have proven these things were alien in origin; human-made things are always so fragile, so quick to fall apart.

⚜

I remember the first time I saw you, some twenty-five years back, at an arts festival on Main Street. The way you were dressed, with a smock, heavy pants, and heat-resistant gloves, you looked like you'd stepped out of the past, a blacksmith. You stood in front of a furnace holding a long metal pole, and when you pulled it out, a glowing ball of molten glass hung on the tip. You turned the pole around and around as you made your way to the table, and then you rolled the molten tip in a pile colored glass, the colors melting beau-tifully. Finally, you took the pipe and blew into it, the liquid glass growing with your breath, your neck reddening, the veins standing out as you blew, and as I stood there watching with the rest of the crowd, I wondered what it would be like to touch that neck, the warm pulsing vein, move my hand up higher to the stubble of your jaw, your cheek, what it would be like to rub my own cheek against yours.

I stayed even after you finished your demonstration and the crowd walked away. I wandered over to the display table, where you had some pieces for sale. I grabbed the first thing I saw, which I later found out was a pipe for smoking weed. I didn't smoke at all then, but a few months later, when we began dating, we used it a few times sitting on the roof of your apartment, and then many years later we used it again when our son was a toddler and we were trying to get the spark back, and we lay together on the lawn behind our tiny house looking at the stars, touching each other, wondering how we got so old, not realizing how young we still were.

You had taken off your gloves to ring me up. Your hands were large and dirty, nails clipped short. When I handed you cash for the pipe, our hands brushed, and I noticed how hot your skin felt, as if the fire had seeped underneath it. You told me to come by your store sometime. I raised and lowered my eyes, said I would. And that was the beginning of our story.

                                    ❦

By fall, the "Flock to the Rock" group had split into two factions: those who believed the obelisks were proof of our goodness, a gift from God; and those who claimed the opposite, that they were a mark of evil and associated with America's sins (which, in their minds, had more to do with promiscuity and homosexuality than, say, the genocide and slavery on which the country was built). This group claimed the obelisks marked the end of the world; soon the sinners would be struck down and the worthy rewarded. Neither group entertained the idea that the structures came from aliens, though, so at least they agreed on that.

Of course, there were other theories floating around. There was a vocal group who spoke about the Deep State, who claimed the obelisks were just the latest government attempt to control us. There were the alien enthusiasts, who saw the obelisks as proof of alien life, though they disagreed about the actual purpose of the structures. (Were they a type of technology? A way to surveil us? A weapon? Were the obelisks themselves extraterrestrial life forms? Where were the actual aliens, anyway?)

Then there were those who watched the news, read the articles, listened to people talk in the grocery stores, and still didn't know what to believe, what to feel, except sad that everyone was fighting all the time. There were those who didn't care because they were so wrapped up in the little dramas of their own lives. And there were those who *couldn't* care because they were working three jobs and still struggling to pay rent or because their sons were dying in the streets. None of these problems left when the obelisks arrived; it's just that some people stopped paying attention to them, and they were replaced in the national conversation with something easier to swallow.

❧

When I was young, my parents used to take me to Blockbuster to rent movies on Friday nights. It was the only business left in a run-down strip mall, and my dad called it "the last Blockbuster at the end of the world." Of course, this was before the entire chain went out of business, before pandemics and quarantine, before obelisks. In the alien movies we rented, often starring Will Smith, all the countries in the world put their conflicts aside when faced with a common enemy. It seemed so simple: the path to peace on earth was a violent invasion by an alien species. As I grew up, I understood how far removed from real life movies were—but still, part of me was surprised at the way things turned out after the obelisks arrived, not just in our country, but between you and me.

You and I watched the news together sometimes, but more often we sat on opposite sides of the couch and scrolled through our phones, reading articles from various sites or browsing the comments sections on social media. At first, we scoffed at the same things, rolled our eyes, shared concerns about the rising tension in our town, our country. We didn't talk about it much with our son, who, being a teenager, was mostly wrapped up in his own life, starting senior year of high school, breaking up and getting back together with his boyfriend, staying out too late and coming home smelling faintly like pot.

As the fall wore on, though, you began to repeat some talking points from the conspiracy theorists. I laughed them off at first, but soon you were repeating them more often, almost every evening when we plopped down on the couch after dinner. It wasn't until Halloween night that I realized you were serious. Our ranch house was across from a cornfield on a lonely country road, but there were several cross streets, so we got a good amount of trick-or-treaters each year. This year, alien costumes dominated. We sat on the porch and sipped some spiked cider as the chill of dusk came on. After the most recent group of alien kids had left our step, you shook your head.

"Shame, kids being brainwashed."

I asked what you meant, and you launched into a diatribe I had heard before, but never from you. They're teaching kids that aliens are real, you said, but won't talk about God in school. Kids are being taught to worship the wrong thing. They're growing up with loose morals. You stopped there, and I looked at you skeptically. I wanted to say, Are you not the same man who owns a glassware store that sometimes sells bongs to underage teens? But more trick-or-treaters arrived, and the conversation dropped. We spent the rest of the night giving out candy and watching the moon rise in silence.

You ended up going to bed early that night while I stayed up watching scary movies, which had always been a ritual of ours. One of the movies was *Invasion of the Body Snatchers*, which made me think of aliens, which made me think of you. I felt a shift in our relationship, a new distance that wasn't there before. I stayed up after the movie was over, sitting by an open window that let in the fall breeze, waiting for our son to come home, thinking how much I missed the days of trick-or-treating with him. When he finally came in the door, I was surprised to see him in costume. He was wearing big feathery wings and had glitter all over his body. I laughed.

"I didn't know you dressed up! Are you an angel?"

He laughed too, said, "I'm an alien, Mom, can't you tell?"

❧

As fall wore on, you started taking days off work to visit the nearby obelisk. That in itself didn't bother me, except I knew you went there to argue. You often came home still angry, and one time you were brought home by the police.

Then, the night before Thanksgiving, you didn't come home at all. At first, I wasn't worried. Our son was out too, with his boyfriend, and I relished the quiet. By the time our son came home, though, I was getting worried. What if something had happened to you? When you arrived in the midmorning, you smelled like booze and campfire. I was pissed.

"We were trying to set them straight," you said.

"Who's *we*? Who's *them*?"

You didn't answer. "Those people don't have a clue. They're worshipping these things as if they're something good."

I was standing at the counter, chopping celery for the stuffing. "How do you know they're not?" I stopped chopping and looked at you. "How do you know anything?"

Your eyes flitted from angry to hurt and back again. I knew I had said the wrong thing. You told me once you were insecure about the fact that I had gone to college and you had not, that you became an apprentice glassblower after high school and I had gone to school to study and make art and become a teacher.

"It's in the Bible," you replied coldly. "Read it sometime."

I shook my head, opened my mouth to apologize or call you an asshole, but then you continued: "These people, all these years, acting like their behavior would never catch up with them. But it has.

All the sex, all the abortions, all the gays and trans and all the fucking libs who say they're *woke* but are really more asleep than anyone else."

I stared at you in disbelief. I'd never heard you say anything like that before. I gave you a moment to realize what you said, to catch yourself. You didn't.

"You do remember," I said, shaking, trying to hold back my rage, "that our son is one of those *gays*, right?"

I saw the anger in your eyes falter, transform into sheepishness, guilt. But that shame made you defensive, and you raised your voice. "Yeah, well, I didn't mean him. He's not like the rest."

"What does that even mean?" I cried. I realized I still had the knife in my hand and threw it in the sink with a clatter.

Our son must have heard because he came downstairs, rubbing his eyes. He stood in the foyer like a child just woken from a nap. "What's going on?" he asked, his voice small. He wasn't used to this. We had never been a shouting family.

"Everything's fine," I said. I tried to smile but felt my lips trembling, so I turned my back.

You went outside to the shed. I continued chopping the celery, wondering what was happening to us, what had just been broken.

❧

We went weeks without speaking, avoiding eye contact as we passed one another in the hallway. I tried to put on a cheerful face for the students in my class, but as winter came on, I was feeling defeated. After all this time, was it really over? I started looking up apartment rentals nearby. As I was scrolling through listings, I came upon your old apartment, the one you lived in when we first met, above the bar on Main Street. How strange, after all that time, to see inside the rooms again. It looked different, new paint and floors, but there were the same old radiators, the same old windows from which we watched drunk college kids fight and fall in love a hundred times a night.

Seeing that old apartment gave me pause. I stopped looking through rentals, but I bookmarked a few. I wasn't giving up on the idea completely. But then, later that night, I was cleaning out my closet, and I came across the glass birds. You made me the first one, a hummingbird, in our first weeks of dating, gave it to me with a tag attached, on which you had written in messy script: *My heart beats fast as hummingbird wings around you.* The second one, a bluebird, you presented to me in the hospital the day after I gave birth to our son, when I was still ragged and crying. The third one was a cardinal. You made it for me after I had my miscarriage. She would have been a girl. I think you meant to give me hope, that our daughter was out there somewhere, the old idea that when you see a cardinal it's a visit from a loved one. But it was too soon after the miscarriage and reminded me too much of what I had lost, so I had taken it, along with the other two birds, and placed them at the back of the closet, where they'd been now for so many years.

I picked up the hummingbird. One of its wings had broken off, and I cursed myself for being so careless, for forgetting how delicate your glasswork was.

⚘

I looked into marriage counseling, but every place I called was booked solid for months. It seemed the national argument over the obelisks was infiltrating many other marriages besides ours. One day, you found me at the kitchen table, crying, phone in hand. For the first time in weeks, you spoke to me, asked me what was wrong. When I told you I was looking into marriage counseling but couldn't find us an appointment, something in your face softened. You sat down and apologized, sincerely, for what you had said. You didn't know what came over you. It was like all the other voices you'd been listening to took over. You were sorry. You loved me. You loved our son. You looked at me hard when you said that, your eyes shining. I took your hand.

After that, we had a few good weeks that turned into a few good months, but as it got closer to the one-year anniversary of the obelisks' arrival, things started falling apart again. There were rumors of people disappearing. People left their beds in the middle of the night, were seen wandering close to the obelisks, and then were just gone. After the first dozen or so disappeared, it became clear there was a pattern. They were all women. Most of them were middle-aged or older, although there were a couple in their teens and twenties. In the scramble to come up with an explanation, some media outlets framed it as an abduction. The alien believers claimed the aliens were using women to start a new race of alien-human hybrids. The "Flock to the Rock" group was confused. It was possible the women had ascended in Rapture, but they were just ordinary women, many who didn't even go to church. And what about all the good men who deserved to be chosen as well? The group you had been following, who looked at the obelisks as a sign of the apocalypse, went back to sin, as always: These women were daughters of Eve, and their disappearance was a warning of what would happen if we didn't repent.

No one considered the possibility that the women weren't taken. That they just left.

❦

Soon you began spending nights at the obelisk again, camping out, arguing with the other men there, absorbing the hate speech of makeshift preachers. You stopped going to work. At first I thought you were just taking time off, but then you told me the shop was closing. The economy was tanking. People were too busy fighting to care. People started putting signs in their windows, some saying *Take me!*, others warning about the dangers of sin, others promising people like our son they would burn in hell. I saw fistfights erupt in parking lots. I saw children come into my classroom hungry, frazzled from their parents' fighting. I brought granola bars for them and talked to the guidance counselor, but she was overwhelmed.

I tried to take refuge in art, but I wasn't inspired. The paintings I made of the obelisks turned out like flat black trapezoids. I couldn't capture their energy, the way they glowed. Our son came out to the shed one afternoon, watched me work, saw me throw my paintbrush down in frustration. He came up behind and hugged me, and I thought we must have done something right, having raised a son so gentle.

He and I had a long talk that night. He talked about how scared he was, threats shouted at him from passing pickups. He didn't want to stay here anymore. I told him that was okay, I'd always known— I'd always *hoped*—he'd leave Ohio for college. But he shook his head, said no. He wanted to go farther. He wanted to go abroad, France. An art school there had accepted him and would pay most of his tuition. I want to be an artist like you, he said. That he saw me that way, as an artist, rather than a wife or a mom or a teacher: I grabbed his hand. I said, of course. No matter what it takes.

The next morning, I woke early ready to start something new. A sculpture. I worked on it in the yard. If there were aliens watching us, I wanted them to be able to see it. At first, I didn't know what I was making. I felt my way forward, let the materials lead me. I used found objects, scrap metal in the yard, old bicycle parts, old toys, old siding, bottles and brush and buttons. At the end of the first day, I was sore and still didn't know what the sculpture would become.

When you stopped home that night to make yourself a sandwich, you asked what that monstrosity was in the yard. I didn't answer, and you didn't come to bed.

❧

You wanted to destroy the obelisks. There was a handful of other likeminded men in town, and you'd been talking with them about doing it. You admitted this to me with a kind of pride. I shook my head, laughed it off; there was no way you'd do such a thing. But as the weeks went on, I began to doubt my belief in you. You were becoming a stranger. Who knew what you were capable of?

You weren't home much anymore, but when you were, our son avoided you. In your hurt over this, I could see a sliver of your old self. I told you his plans to go abroad for school; I'd already used our savings to pay for room and board and book his flight for the day after graduation. I expected some kind of pushback from you; after all, as his father, you should have been part of this conversation. But the obelisks were all-consuming. You simply shot me a wounded look, shrugged, said, Good for him, and went back to your furious scrolling.

You were gone for days. I continued to work on my sculpture. I realized, halfway through, that I was making a bird. I was surprised: over the years, birds had become a symbol of our love, a love that, as far as I could tell, was gone. But then I remembered birds had not always been a symbol of *us*. I had loved birds long before I met you. I loved the way they existed in two worlds. I was terrified of flying in planes, but I had recurring dreams where I soared above the earth, above cornfields and canyons. I always woke up before I fell.

❧

On the one-year anniversary of the obelisk's appearance, there was an explosion in the cornfield. Dozens of people were arrested, a few were hurt, and the rest were ordered off the site. The obelisk, of course, was unharmed. The police roped it off again with yellow tape.

You called me from jail. I swear I didn't do it, you said. I reminded you of our previous conversation. You said that was just talk, you wouldn't have really done it, you wouldn't have risked hurting anyone. Your voice was sincere, so I agreed to come pick you up. You apologized the whole ride home, like a teenage boy being picked up from a party where the older kids had been drinking.

"That blast," you said, "it woke me up. I could have died, for what? I don't want to leave you. I don't want to leave our son."

You reached out and touched my thigh, and it shot the usual warmth up to my groin. Still, I couldn't forget everything you had said. The distance between us was still there. Maybe you were returning to the man you were before, but I couldn't return with you.

We pulled into the driveway, headlights flooding the yard, spotlighting my sculpture.

"Oh," you said, and took my hand. "It's a bird."

I nodded, let my hand rest in yours for a moment, but I knew the bird didn't mean the same thing to both of us.

❦

A couple years after I graduated college, we had a long-distance relationship. It lasted almost a year. I had to go back home to New York because my dad had cancer, and I wanted to help my mom take care of him. In the months before I left, things weren't great between us. We'd been dating about four years, and our relationship had stagnated. Every night after work we got together, ate takeout, watched TV, and attempted to have sex, though most of the time we were too tired. Then I would either go back to my apartment in the middle of the night or squeeze next to you on your twin mattress. I was frustrated that you weren't growing up. You were frustrated that our life together was no longer a party. We fought. We considered seeing other people. And then my dad was dying, and I was leaving. I thought it was over. Instead, you proposed the night before I left.

You didn't go down on one knee; you backed up a little as if you were afraid of me, and it was the first time I had seen you scared like that. As you stood there holding the ring, silver with a tiny sapphire stone, I realized I had power over you, and that power frightened me but it emboldened me too, made it easier for me to forgive you for all our past fights. Even now, the memory of the fear in your eyes that night allows me to forgive you again, to keep forgiving you even though I am farther away from you than ever before.

I still left for New York, but with the ring on my finger. I was there almost a year, and the ring kept us together because we knew on the other side we'd be starting a new life, our grown-up life, together. You came to visit sometimes, drove ten hours to sit with me at my dad's bedside. But mostly we talked on the phone, texted, emailed, wrote letters. My heart always jumped when I saw one of yours in the mailbox. My mom laughed, teasing: So old-fashioned! But those letters were what got us through that time, that distance.

And that's kind of what this is: A love letter from very, very, very far away.

The night I brought you home from jail, you willingly slept on the couch, a kindness. I woke up in the middle of the night and knew there was something I had to do. I went into our son's room and looked at his sleeping face, his hands big like puppy paws, his curls splayed on the pillow. I kissed his cheek, as I used to when he was a baby.

Downstairs, you were sleeping, a mirror image of our son. I kissed you too. Then I went outside. In the moonlight the metal pieces of my sculpture glinted like jewels. I knew *what* I made—a big metal bird—but still didn't know *why* I made it. My whole life, I never really knew why I made art; it was just an impulse. It occurred to me that it could be the same for the obelisks. All this time, everyone thinking of the obelisks as some kind of message or weapon. But what if they were just art from another world?

I needed to go see it. And I wanted to bring my sculpture too, place it beside the obelisk, like starting a conversation. I lifted the bird, with difficulty, into the bed of the truck, and then I drove slowly down the road to the cornfield. It was quiet, no cars around, the houses mostly dark, though here and there the glow of dim lamplight spilled out from behind a downstairs window. I thought of all the people sleeping in these houses, how quiet they finally were, and I wondered where everyone went in their dreams. I remembered my mother's sleeping face, how after a long day she sometimes fell asleep on the couch, the skin pulled tight across her nose and cheeks, her mouth open, snoring slightly, how far away she seemed. She died a few years back, during the pandemic. I wondered where she was now. And all those women who had disappeared, where had they gone?

When I made it to the cornfield, I saw the yellow tape roping off the obelisk. No one else was there; after the explosion, everyone had been evacuated, and no one risked coming back. I pulled the truck as close as I could and then wheeled my sculpture on a dolly over to where the obelisk stood. My bird was dwarfed by the imposing trapezoid and looked inelegant, messy, all-too human. Still, it felt right to leave it there.

What happened next is hard to explain, but I need you to understand: I wanted to go.

It started with a warmth emanating from the obelisk, which felt like sunlight, like lying on the beach as a teenager. Then there was a tingle. It started at the back of my neck and traveled down my spine, and then all the hairs on my body were standing on end.

Then there was light.

It came from above, underneath, behind, around me. It was blinding, and in that blindness I saw you and our son, I saw my parents, I saw my students and friends and neighbors and all our old dogs, all the apartments and houses we'd lived in, even my baby girl, and it was like I was saying goodbye, but I didn't feel like I was going away from something, I felt like I was going toward something.

And then I was above the earth, flying for the first time outside of dreams, and I could see below me the sculpture grow smaller and smaller until it was the size of a real hummingbird, and the obelisks shrunk in the distance to the size of pebbles, and the arguments over them seemed small, petty, of little consequence, forgivable from so far away.

The stars were so numerous and so bright. It was strange to think these were the same stars I gazed at while camping with my dad as a child, the same stars we watched from your roof when we were young and in love, the same stars I got to glance at only sometimes as an older woman while walking the dog or taking out the trash. They were so close now. I reached out my hand to touch them, but instead a floating obelisk appeared in front of me. It was mute, but I felt it asking me a question, giving me a choice. And—forgive me—I chose to go.

I cannot describe to you adequately the speed at which I was rushed inside. I cannot describe the beings that populate the obelisk, I cannot tell you if they are aliens, or angels, or something else entirely. I cannot tell you who was right. I can only tell you it doesn't matter. The other women who disappeared, they are here also, and

they are happy. We are happy. But that doesn't mean we don't sometimes look down on Earth and miss it, miss you.

I see you there, with our son, gazing at my sculpture next to the
obelisk. It looks like you're standing at my grave, mourning me. But I
know that's not what's happening. I can see you looking at me through
the bird, through the obelisk. I can see you reaching out your hand
to touch the structure, and when you do, this is the message you will
receive, and with your next heartbeat you will understand everything.

WHEN THE TREE GROWS
THIS HIGH

Maissie Burns was eighteen years old when her father found her a betrothed. His name was Ewan Glas, her father said, a nice boy who lived just outside the village. Boy? He's young, her father said, so you'll have to wait until he reaches sixteen to marry. How long was she to wait? Two years, her father said.

So he was fourteen years old. Fourteen! Maissie remembered when she was that age, just a child, still playing with dolls, still wearing feedsack dresses over pantaloons. It wasn't until late in her fourteenth year that her first blood came, and with it long skirts that once belonged to her dead mother, as well as the expectation of marriage and children. But four years had passed since that day, and still she had not married because she had not felt ready, and her father, a soft touch for his only child, had given in and allowed her to remain at home after she finished school. It was helpful to have her there, after all. Then, in the spring of her eighteenth year, something bloomed inside her, and she told her father she was ready and he agreed and began searching for eligible suitors, preferably a man with at least a little money, for they had none. The men, though, began to leave when the Great War started that summer, and all through autumn they continued to leave, family after family bereft of marriageable sons, until all they were left with were young boys and old men, and Maissie had begged her father not to marry her to the old fishmonger who always stared at her with such strange eyes in the market. And so they were left with this: this young man, Ewan, from one of the few other Catholic families around their small village south of Port Glasgow, still in school and destined to take over his father's sheep farm someday, when he was fully grown.

⁊₭

Maissie met him for the first time a month later, after midnight Mass on Christmas Eve. Maissie had been nervous the whole week leading up to the meeting, not in the way she'd heard described in love poems, not out of some desire to impress or out of any desire at all, but because she was afraid she was going to meet her husband, and he was going to be a scrawny, pimply-faced boy, uncouth, like a little brother whom she would one day have to bed. As she sat beside her father in the pew, she could not pay attention to what the priest was saying. The church was even emptier than usual, so many of the young men gone. Because of this, it was easy to spot Ewan, sitting near the front with his parents and little brother.

She studied him. She could see only the back of his head, thick, nut-brown hair that curled at the ends. He was not quite as tall as his father, but he was a couple inches taller than his mother, probably about the same height as Maissie. At least from this angle, he did not look so young. She could even imagine him turning around and having the face of a soldier, like some of the boys she'd known from school who'd been shipped off to war.

After church, outside in the cold, the stars sharp in the sky above them, she finally saw his face. It was not pimply, nor was there anything disagreeable about it. Their parents introduced them and they both said hello, and that was it. His voice was contralto, soft and gentle, not the high voice of a child nor the breaking timbre of a boy just entering the pains of puberty. He seemed shy, perhaps even more nervous than she, and looked up at her only twice, then quickly lowered his eyes again. She couldn't be sure in the dark, but it looked like they were brown. She liked brown eyes. She felt her body loosen a bit.

They stood outside the church shivering while Maissie's father spoke with Ewan's parents. Side by side old couples bereft of their sons exited the church, women in headscarves wiping their eyes and clutching their crosses, holding onto their last prayer. Ewan's little brother played peek-a-boo, hiding behind Ewan's legs, peeking out at Maissie, laughing. Ewan and Maissie laughed too, looked at each other for just a few seconds longer. Soon it began to snow, small flakes falling into Ewan's hair and settling there like nesting birds, unmelting.

※

Maissie did not see Ewan again until spring. She was walking home from work, trying to enjoy the fragrance of the flowering trees but finding she couldn't. She walked with her head bent, troubled by the contrast between spring's beauty and the death she was surrounded by in the tailor shop. She had been working at her father's shop since she left school and had grown accomplished for a girl with no real training, her mother having passed shortly after giving birth to her, her father offering instruction only in the basics. She had taught herself the finer points: how to trim lace on the edge of a veil, how to sew tiny buttons on baby clothes, how to embroider a cross on an infant's baptismal gown. But all these tasks had been overtaken by one job that she did not enjoy at all: sewing shrouds for the dead.

She had done it before, of course, here and there. People died. But since the Great War started, it felt like all she did was sew shrouds. The bodies of the young men from her village and the neighboring villages were returning one after another, their burials back to back. The thought of these dead young men, many of whom she knew from school or from the village, threw a dark veil over everything, even the trees, with their frothy white blossoms like wedding dresses. Those boys would never see another spring. She thought resentfully of a village to the east which she'd heard had lost none of their soldiers thus far. The dark veil seemed to pass over her own heart then, when she thought, ashamedly, *Just wait. Just wait.*

And then, as she was passing by the schoolyard, the sun hanging low in the sky, she saw Ewan. She crossed to the other side of the road, hoping he wouldn't see her, but there was no need. He was too involved in his game of handball, which he was playing with half a dozen other boys. She may not have even recognized him except that she remembered his hair, the way it curled at the ends and fell over his eyes. She watched him as she walked, noticed how big his hands and feet were, like puppy paws. Despite this, he moved his body with such grace through the scraggled yellow grass of the schoolyard that it brought tears to Maissie's eyes. She hurriedly wiped them and interrogated herself. No, it wasn't because she was falling in love with this boy. It was this: She wanted him to remain a boy. She didn't want him growing up quickly just to marry her. She didn't want to steal his youth. Too many young men were already having their youth stolen from them.

She went home, lay in her bed and cried, and when her father came home an hour later, she told him: I can't do it. Why did you have to match me with someone so young? Her father, as always, was sympathetic. He wanted her to be happy. Didn't she want a family of her own one day? Of course he knew she did; having grown up without a mother, the one thing she wanted in life was to become a mother herself. But that life seemed unimaginable now, surrounded as they were by death and more death.

He put his arm around her. What will make you happy?

But it wasn't about happiness anymore. There was something else. Duty. Sacrifice. Words she had known but had never fully grasped. Maybe I will be a nurse, she said. Maybe I can join the war effort.

She felt her father's body stiffen. Then he sighed, a sigh that turned into a coughing fit that lasted a full minute. Maissie turned to him, concerned. I'm fine, he said. But go see Nancy first. Go see her, and then decide.

꽃

The following week, Maissie went to visit her old friend, who had just returned after serving as a nurse since the war's start. Nancy was a quiet girl, a good Catholic, so it made sense that she would spend her life trying to serve others rather than herself. Nancy's mother brought them tea as they sat side by side on the porch steps. There was something empty and undone in her friend's eyes that frightened Maissie, so she did not press her to speak, and they sat in silence most of the visit. But right when Maissie got up to leave, Nancy grabbed her arm. It's not worth it, she said. There's nothing you can do. Those men, they're lost. They die so easily. I never knew how fragile men were! She paused, and then continued in a softer voice: The worst is their eyes, their faraway eyes. Even in the hospital, they're still stuck in the trenches, and there's nothing you can do to pull them out. Even if they live through the war, they all die there, in those trenches.

Maissie embraced her. She expected her friend to cry in her arms like she had done years ago when someone hurt her feelings at school. But Nancy remained limp, simply allowed Maissie to hold her for a moment and then quickly broke away, saying she had to help her mother with supper.

On the walk home, Maissie thought about what her friend had said. She expected Nancy's words to wear her down, but on the contrary, they made her stronger. She was going to do it. She would leave home, become a nurse. She would not wait around to marry. Instead of sewing shrouds for young men, she would save them.

When she arrived home, she looked for her father to tell him the news but could not find him. Finally, she opened his bedroom door and found him lying in bed, burning up, delirious, his breath wheezing in and out. Father, she said. He looked through her and called her by her mother's name, Fiona, and he continued to murmur *Fiona* as she took care of him that night, stroking his forehead with wet rags, holding a bowl of steaming camphor under his chin, feeding him soup and honeyed tea.

The delirium had passed by morning, and he remembered her name again, but the fever persisted, as did the ragged, labored breathing. While he was resting, Maissie ran to get the doctor, a kind-eyed acquaintance of her father, who followed her home and took stock of his condition. Pneumonia, he finally said, his face grave. Given your father's age, this could be dangerous. You will need to be at your father's side.

And so she was. Instead of becoming a soldier's nurse, she played nurse to her father, administering the tincture provided by the doctor, not a cure, but something to clear his lungs. Only time will tell, the doctor said. And time passed, weeks, then a month, then two. Because the tailor shop was closed, they had very little money or food. They survived on the kindness of neighbors, a basket arriving on the doorstep every day, from whom Maissie did not know, until one day she saw two figures walking away from the door, a woman and a young man with nut-brown hair that curled at the tips.

Eventually, Maissie was able to help her father to his feet, and by summer he was well enough to begin working in the tailor shop again, but something about him had slowed. He needed her. And so the notion of becoming a war nurse flickered away from her.

At summer's end, her father told her he had a surprise, and she followed him out to the front yard. He presented her with the sapling of an apple tree. He had placed it, the roots in a burlap sack, beside another tree, one that had been there the whole of Maissie's life. I planted that the week after you were born, he said, in honor of your mother. This apple tree, we will plant in honor of your new life, to mark the time you must wait. When the tree grows this high—he held his hand up to his heart—you will be wed.

A few inches, then. That was all. A few inches and she would be a married woman, married to a boy she hardly knew.

⁂

By next summer, the summer of 1916, the tree was chest-high, and Ewan was sixteen, but the wedding was delayed because Ewan's father had gone off to war in spring after the British government passed the Military Service act, conscripting all eligible men in Scotland. Initially, married men had been exempt, but the rule was changed in May, so Ewan's father was obliged to go. Maissie's own father had been spared both because he was a widower with a child still at home and because of his age. Ewan's father was only thirty-four, had married young in the way of the village. It was easy to blame conscription, but Ewan's uncles had volunteered the previous year and then died in the trenches; Maissie had sewn their shrouds. Ewan's father promised he'd make it home to his wailing wife and silent sons. But only a month later, Maissie sewed his shroud too.

Ewan had left school when his father left for war, and he took over the family farm with his mother's help. It was supposed to be temporary, but now, with his father dead, Ewan was sixteen years old and in charge of thirty acres and one hundred sheep. Maissie felt sorry for Ewan. She knew what it was like to lose a parent, though she couldn't remember the losing, just the constant state of loss that had followed her like a shadow ever since.

There was a funeral, which Maissie attended with her father: church service, burial, and then a reception at Ewan's home. It was the first time she'd been there. The main farmhouse was large and time-worn white, with several cottages and outbuildings dotting the rolling hills like lost sheep. The sheep themselves were penned in a large area away from the main house, which Maissie and her father passed on their way. Inside the house, Ewan's mother, all in black, sat in a chair silently, staring straight ahead, not crying, and beside her stood her two sons, the small one and Ewan.

How much he had changed since she'd last seen him! His jaw more defined, with a hint of stubble that she could sense would one day be a full, red-brown beard. His shoulders too, filled out, broad under his black jacket. It was like seeing the ghost of his father. She could still see his youth in his eyes, in the shyness of his glance, but there was something else there now, a sadness that made him look older.

Maissie and her father approached the family and offered their condolences. Ewan's mother tried to smile as she thanked them, but Maissie could see her lips quivering. She clutched both her sons' hands so tightly their fingertips were blue. Suddenly she let go of Ewan's hand. Why don't you take Maissie for a walk? Ewan looked surprised but agreed, gesturing Maissie to follow him.

They walked out of the dim house into the bright day. It was beautiful, the blue sky brushed with cirrus clouds, the green hills draped with heather and wild thyme, the fragrance of which rolled down the hills and mingled with the scent of manure. This was the first time Maissie had been alone with Ewan, or with any boy. The silence was not uncomfortable. But then Maissie remembered why they were here in the first place, and she felt guilty for enjoying the sun on her skin when Ewan's father would never see the sun again. She knew she was supposed to believe that Ewan's father, and all those who'd died, were bathed in eternal light, but she could only imagine them buried in the trenches. Heaven seemed so unreal, while this earth with its sun was the paradise. So what kind of hope for salvation was there?

Ewan asked if she would like to see the sheep. She said she would, and he led her to the pen. Ewan opened the gate to let Maissie go in first. The sheep, eating and sleeping and wandering, seemed not to notice them.

So you take care of all these sheep? she asked, and immediately regretted it. He was silent for a moment and then said, Yes. My uncle and my mother have been helping. My father just started the shearing before he left. I haven't been able to finish yet, on my own.

I'm sorry, she started to say, but he shook his head. Don't be, he said. I'm glad to take over. This farm's been in my family hundreds of years. When I'm out here, I feel a connection to my kin. It's like all those people, they're all still living through the land. My da, too.

Maissie didn't know what to say, but his words felt wise, much wiser than she would have imagined such a young man to be. In silence, they watched a lamb wobble over to its mother and begin suckling. There was something here, she thought, some kind of answer to her question.

❧

It wasn't until the following summer that they were wed, when Ewan was seventeen and Maissie twenty-one. She wore her mother's dress, which had also been her grandmother's. Her father altered it and presented it to her on the morning of her wedding, tears in his eyes. The white was yellowed slightly around the hem, but Maissie preferred it that way; it reminded her that other women had done this, had left their parents, had married men they barely knew, and sometimes they must have been happy.

It had been two months since she had last seen Ewan, and standing beside him in church she realized how tall he was, at least two heads above her now. His hair still curled at the bottom, and his beard was filling in. It was red-brown, as she had imagined it would be. When he kissed her gently at the end of the ceremony, she felt the beard tickle her chin, and she almost giggled but did not want him feel as if the kiss had been silly in some way. It wasn't. It was the third time in her life she'd been kissed, but the first time she'd ever been kissed like that. Tenderly.

That night, she stood before him in her nightgown. I am not sure what to do, she said, laughing nervously. Me either, he said, and she could see the deep flush in his cheeks as his eyes grazed her and then landed back on the floor. We could just hold each other, she suggested.

So that's what they did, that night and the next and for many weeks and months after, lying side by side in bed, not quite like siblings because she felt a stirring inside her that she knew was not sisterly. Still, she kept to her side of the bed because she wasn't sure if he felt the same stirring. How tired they were, too, after a long day in the fields, so when night came sometimes sleep was the only thing they desired.

Ewan's hands grew rough, his forearms strong and large. He was changing from something pliant to something sturdy. She was, too. They had a sweet Christmas together, huddled around the fireplace in the main house with his mother and her father, while his younger brother played with a train set around the Christmas tree. Later, in their cottage that dotted the hills a quarter mile from the main house, Ewan presented Maissie with a shawl he had made himself from the spring wool. My mother helped, he admitted. As they held each other in the cold that night, she considered turning to him, but she was still afraid he might not want what she wanted.

The new year came and went, and then Ewan's birthday. She surprised him with a quilt she had been working on for months, patterned with greens and blues, which she had found out from his mother were his favorite colors. She had sewn some secrets into the quilt: a scrap from the dress she had worn when she first met him; an infinity symbol sewn into one square, a heart into another. That night they huddled under the quilt and held each other close, but still she was afraid to turn to him and tell him what she wanted.

Perhaps they could not officially call themselves husband and wife because they had not yet consummated their marriage, but they were happy. And then their happiness was cut short: two weeks after his eighteenth birthday, in February of 1918, Ewan was conscripted for military service. He flinched when he found out, nothing more. Maissie cried and begged him not to go, and when he told her that he had to, there was no way around it, she ran to her father, who held her as she sobbed. It will be okay, he told her. The tide is turning, the war will be over soon. You have to be strong for him.

When she got back to the cottage, Ewan was sitting by the fire. He jumped up, took her hands. I was worried, he said. Are you okay? She looked in his eyes, kind and brown, and felt such warmth for this man—a man for certain now, not a boy—concerned about her when it was she who should be concerned for him.

That night, as they lay together, she couldn't sleep. She shuddered as she breathed, and she could feel him behind her doing the same. Finally, she felt him move closer to her, rise against her, and she

moved herself back to rub against him and could feel her own wetness staining her nightgown, which she lifted then, to let him slide
in, and it was that simple, surprisingly easy despite the first snap of
pain. And they slept after, soundly.

She spent the next day in anticipation of night, anxious to lay
her body next to his again. She marveled at his gentleness. His hands
were so unlike any other man she'd known, the rough hands of her
great uncle who had touched her in a way she hadn't liked when
she was a child, the hands of the boy who had grabbed her jaw after
graduation and stuck his tongue in her mouth. Ewan's gentle hands
were on her again that night, and the night after, and her hands were
on him too, full of his hair, his beard, his broad back. So drunk was
she with this new dream of love that she barely remembered Ewan
was leaving for the war. But the day came, and he left, and suddenly
her hands were empty again.

⚜

To fill them, Maissie sheared sheep, grabbing handfuls of wool
thick as storm clouds, and she caught newborn lambs as they fell
from their mothers' bodies. She touched her own belly, wondering.
But her blood came and her belly never grew, so she had to content
herself with the lambs, bottle-feeding the ones rejected by the ewes.

The work of the farm was hard, but she did not have to shoulder
it herself. Her father came to help some days, when work in the tailor
shop was slow. Ewan's one surviving uncle would stop by here and
there, too, but he had his own farm to run. Mostly, Maissie's help
came in the form of women: her mother-in-law, and the wives of
Ewan's dead uncles, and other widows from the village. These wom-
en worked together to get the farm through spring and into early
summer, shearing sheep, gathering wool, feeding the animals and

cleaning their pens, mending fences, tending the garden, cradling orphaned lambs like the infants they would never again bear.

Nights, Maissie spent alone in her cottage. Her mother-in-law had offered to let her stay in the main house, and her father, too, offered Maissie could come home. But Maissie felt she had to stay in this cottage, had to continue living this life she had started. She felt herself transforming, arms ropy with muscle, skin sunburnt, hips and breasts filling out as she ate heartily each night, and something inside her was transforming too. So she stayed in the cottage, spent sleepless nights by the fire knitting a sweater for Ewan. He would come back, she promised herself. He would wear this sweater.

And the promise came true, though Ewan did not wear the sweater, because it was June when he was finally granted a short leave to return home. When he arrived, Maissie ran outside barefoot and watched him approach. At first she wasn't sure it was him, he was so changed. Had he gotten taller in the months he'd been gone? She'd been expecting him to come back to her skeletal, but instead he had filled out. His uniform was a wan green-brown like mud after a long spring rain, and his hair was cropped short. As he got closer she saw his jaw sharply defined, the stubble clinging to it like shorn stalks, and his skin was weathered, lips chapped. His eyes, though, were the same brown, kind and shy, but carrying within them a new woundedness.

They stood in front of one another as the clouds shifted above them: sun, shadow, sun shadow. She knew he was assessing her too, and she found herself sharp with longing that he would be pleased with what he saw. It felt as if they were meeting again for the first time. She started to say hello at the same time he did, and they both laughed, and she reached out her hand to take his, but before she could, his mother burst out the door of the main house and came running.

They spent the day in the main house with his mother and little brother and then ate dinner there together, Maissie father's joining them too. Maissie could feel Ewan's heat next to her at the table and it was all she could do to not touch his forearm or his thigh, the muscular spread of it on the chair next to her. She waited until they got back to the cottage, but even then, she held back. They crawled into bed and lay there, unsleeping, for a long time. Out the window, the cicadas sawed and occasionally the bleat of a lamb cut through the drone. Finally, Maissie felt Ewan's hand tentatively circle around her, and she gripped it hard to pull him close, and he moved against her, both of their nightclothes still on. She turned around to face him and felt his chapped lips on hers, and she rubbed the sandpaper of his jaw in her hands and then moved his head to the soft between her breasts and felt the roughness there, and suddenly he was saying things to her, how he missed her, how he wanted her to undress and stand naked before him, and she found herself willing to oblige, but only on the condition that he do the same. Then they were both completely naked, standing before one another on opposite sides of the bed in a darkness constellated by glimmers from the half moon.

Maissie wanted to jump across the bed but held herself back, waiting for him to come to her first, and he did, crawling across the bed to kneel before her and tenderly touch all the parts of her body with his mouth until she couldn't take it anymore and she pushed him down on the bed and straddled him as he grabbed her hips, and for a few moments, then, time and war and death did not exist.

Ewan was home for nine more days, and those days were filled with work: tending the garden, caring for sick sheep, selling lambs to nearby farmers, delivering excess wool to the government center where it would be used to make soldiers' uniforms. As they worked, Maissie and Ewan stole looks at each other across the sheep pen. Every night after dinner in the main house, they walked back to the cottage holding hands and immediately went to bed, even though it was still light out. They used the light to trace every scar, every line, every mark on the other's body, the mole by his belly button, the birthmark under her left breast, right above her heart.

And then he had to leave. That morning, they did not speak. Everything they needed to tell each other was spoken through their bodies: I love you. I'll miss you. Please don't forget me.

᪾

The following month, Maissie found herself too sick in the morning to work. While she apologized profusely to her mother-in-law, the woman beamed and embraced her. Maissie was confused only for a moment, and then it dawned on her. She had missed her monthly blood. She was pregnant.

She wrote to Ewan. She wrote him letters each week of the pregnancy, describing the nausea, the strange dreams she was having, the slow growth of her belly, but she never heard back. Summer shifted to autumn, the crops ready for harvest, the sheep ready for rutting. Maissie knew letters were often delayed, that sometimes a letter might not arrive for months. She knew this, but still she worried.

Maissie spent her days with her mother-in-law and Ewan's widowed aunts, all working together like sisters in an abbey. More than sisters, though, they had become like mothers to her, advising her to put her feet up, massaging her back when it hurt, giving her herbs for nausea and heartburn. In bits and pieces, as they worked, they taught her about childbirth, how to squat and how to breathe, how to hold the infant if the infant isn't latching correctly, how to swaddle and how to increase her milk. Maissie was so wrapped up in this new life about to come into the world that there were moments she almost forgot her fears for Ewan. Almost.

And then, in early November, she received a letter from him. She was five months pregnant. She read it over and over again in her cottage, lit a fire so she could read deep into the night. He was so happy about her pregnancy he could not find the words. He thought about her and their baby every moment of every day. Nothing around him, not the darkness or drudgery or death, could steal his joy. He was walking around with a little pearl hidden in his heart, he wrote, and that's what got him through the tough times.

The next morning, Maissie was awoken by excited cries and cheers out in the field. Ewan's aunts were embracing and weeping with joy when she made her way out to them. The war had ended, they said. It was over. Germany had signed an armistice. The boys were coming home.

Maissie felt a flood of relief, as if a breath she had been holding since Ewan left were finally being let out. She cried and hugged her mother-in-law, her new belly pushing against the woman, who kept thanking God, looking at the sky and the treetops as if searching for his face.

Maissie tried to wait patiently for Ewan's return, but the days were endless. One week, then two. In her impatience she knitted a blanket for the new baby, then another, then a third. And so when she saw a soldier walking across the field one surprisingly warm November day, saw the drab green-brown of the uniform from afar, she broke from the group of women and ran to him, ran the whole length of the field without stopping.

But when she got within several yards of him, she realized it was not Ewan at all. She stopped in her tracks, breathing heavy, and found she couldn't catch her breath. She placed a hand on her belly, looked down at the brown leaves that crunched underfoot as the soldier walked toward her. When he reached her, she was still out of breath and it took a moment to remember her name when he asked. Maissie Burns, she said at first, and then corrected herself. Maissie Glas, she said, and the words thrilled her because it was still so new, and this thrill drowned out the soldier's voice so she had to ask him to repeat himself, and when he did, she went cold.

No, she said, shaking her head. The war is over. Ewan cannot be dead. She just received a letter from him a few weeks ago. The soldier looked at her sympathetically. He'd been in the trenches with Ewan. They were friends. He wanted to tell her personally, didn't want her to hear from some telegram. Ewan did not suffer. He was killed by a grenade during one of the final battles. He helped them win, don't you see?

She barely registered his words. It was a cruel joke. The war was over, how could Ewan be gone? And to have died just before the armistice? No, it must be a mistake. She let the soldier embrace her and then she watched him walk away, down the hill to where the other women were working. When she heard Ewan's mother scream, only then did Maissie know it must be true.

※

Maissie gave birth in early March. The first pang hit her while she was walking back from the sheep pen to her cottage, so empty now. It felt like a knife in her side, and then like a vise. She doubled over. When it passed, she straightened and continued walking, but then she noticed the wetness trickling down her legs. She went back to the cottage, did not want to tell anyone just yet. She paced the long floorboards as dusk settled, counting the minutes between contractions as the women had taught her. When the contractions got closer together, she stood by the window of the cottage and looked at the bruise-colored sky, trying to breathe, and thought about the only two people she wanted with her in this moment, the two people who could not be with her: her mother and Ewan.

She staggered to the main house and told her mother-in-law and aunts what was happening. They exploded in joyful cries and tried to usher her to a bedroom, but she said she wanted to give birth in the cottage. Someone went to call for her father.

Near midnight, the pain had become more intense, the contractions coming quick and hard. Then came a pressure that made her want to push, and so she did, encouraged by the women, one of whom placed a cool rag on her forehead, one of whom held her arms while she squatted, and in that ring of fire, Maissie forgot everything, even herself. Even Ewan.

This forgetting remained even after the baby was placed on her chest, and though she was surrounded by half a dozen women, Maissie saw only one, her baby girl. The child opened her eyes and stared up at her, an intense blue. It was only when her mother-in-law leaned close, removed the rag from her forehead, and asked what she was going to name the child, that Maissie remembered this child had a father, and he was dead.

Pearl, she said, remembering his last letter to her. Her name is Pearl.

❧

Easter was late in the spring of 1919. Pearl was almost two months old. Her eyes, so blue when she was born, had changed over the last month as time rushed on like a river, rushing past Maissie's ears so loud she forgot her grief, but now as the river quieted and the baby began to sleep and the days and nights became separate again, she thought more and more of Ewan as she saw their child's eyes transform from blue to green to hazel and finally to a limpid amber, the color of her father's eyes.

Maissie still found it hard to believe sometimes that she would never see those eyes again, that they were closed forever beneath the dirt of the village graveyard. She had avoided the graveyard since the day of the burial, but she passed by it now as she walked with the other villagers in the Easter Parade. The tradition, which had been discontinued during the war, started up again this year with more fanfare than usual to celebrate the boys who made it home. Those men marched in their uniforms, while the widowed women walked behind them. Following them were children decked out in frilly white dresses and hats, shiny shoes and flower crowns, and at the back of the procession the bagpipers wailed mournfully, melody keening over drone. Along the roadway, villagers lined up. The wives of the soldiers who'd returned stood in fancy dresses, their lips red, flowers pinned to their chests, fanning themselves because they were still so hot with happiness that their husbands had come back to them. These women stood by the roadside in front of the graveyard, where the grass grew long by Ewan's grave. Maissie felt a blade of envy rip through her belly. But then Pearl squirmed in the sling, hungry, and Maissie lifted a nipple to her mouth while Pearl looked at her with those brown eyes, and the wound was healed, at least in part.

She walked on with the procession until she came to her father's house, where he was waiting for her. His hair had transformed over the war years into the pure white of snow, as if he were taking on all the years of old age that the dead boys would never get. He smiled as they approached and held out his arms. Pearl unlatched to gurgle at him, milk dribbling down her chin. He was standing by the apple tree, the one they had planted that day when they had finally decided that, yes, Maissie would marry that young man from the sheep farm. In three years it had grown from heart height to tower over their heads, the branches bearing sweet-smelling blossoms. She leaned closer to admire the blooms with Pearl, whose outstretched hand grasped something globular on the branch. The first fruit, so small, unripened. Maissie took it from her child's grip, held it up to her nose and inhaled. Her father examined the tree, surprised. They'd found the only fruit, so early it seemed formed by magic. He warned Maissie it was not yet ready. Maybe another year, he said, and we'll have a whole harvest of sweet apples.

She took a bite anyway as the procession passed on. The flesh was bitter, so bitter it made tears spring to her eyes. She looked at her daughter through the blur and forced herself to swallow. She took another bite, and another, until she reached the seeds, and then she took the seeds in her mouth, felt the smooth black of them on her tongue like some sort of communion, and let them fall from her pursed lips gently into the dirt.

BI6FOOT

I'VE ALWAYS LIVED WITHIN view of a church steeple. From my childhood apartment to the living room of the duplex where I received my first kiss from the landlord's son to the small split-level my parents were able to buy when I was in high school, there was always a church steeple in the distance. Maybe that's what was missing my first year away at college, all the way across the country in California. When I returned home, the steeple was a comforting sight. Far away, the church looked magical, rising from the pages of a fairytale. Up close, though, one could see the chips in the paint, the cracks in the plaster, the repairs that were so desperately needed.

That's what we did over the summer, my father and me. Since the recession hit two years earlier, he'd been making money fixing up old homes in the area, doing everything from painting to drywall to roof repair. Because I was home from school, my dad enlisted me to help with his new project, restoring the time-bruised Reformed Church—paint, shingles, shoring up the steeple so it would last another hundred years beyond the three hundred it had already been standing.

The first day on the job, I saw it: the truck with the license plate that read BI6FOOT. It was a mid-sized pickup, the generic type one often sees here in our corner of rust-belt Pennsylvania. The bumper was covered with stickers. I BELIEVE, with a shadowy image of Sasquatch. THEY'RE OUT THERE, with the cartoonish face of Bigfoot. BIGFOOT RESEARCH TEAM. A Bigfoot family, an angry Bigfoot giving the middle finger, an even angrier Bigfoot with a speech bubble saying DON'T TREAD ON ME.

I stood there for a long time looking at the truck. At first I chuckled, and then I felt a sort of sad curiosity. I should have been helping my dad haul paint cans, but I stood staring at the I BELIEVE sticker. The truck was empty, parked on the side of the road next to the church. It fascinated me that a person could believe so unwaveringly in what was almost certainly a myth. How could someone have so much faith in Bigfoot when God and even people were so hard to believe in?

My dad called my name, so I grabbed the last two paint cans and went to help him lay drop cloths over the church's rose garden. By the time I looked back, the truck was gone.

※

I saw the BI6FOOT truck again a week later. We were working on the roof now. Many of the shingles had fallen off, but there were a few intact. It reminded me of my mom's chemo hair when she had breast cancer a few years ago, the little patches that clung to her scalp, stubborn. My dad was up on the roof scraping off those remaining shingles, the ones that had weathered the storms, when I spotted the BI6FOOT truck right before it turned the corner. I caught a glimpse of the driver this time—just a dim figure wearing a baseball cap. I called up to my dad.

"See that truck?"

He paused, looked down at me, wiped his forehead. "What truck?"

I pointed, but the truck was already out of sight. "Never mind."
I picked up an errant shingle that had fallen onto the grass, chucked
it onto the tarp with the rest. "Just a truck covered with Bigfoot
stickers."

"Huh," he grunted. "Yeah, there's a group around here that goes
hunting for Bigfoot. Call themselves the Sasquatch Society." He
coughed, spit. "Funny what people will believe."

I thought about him and Mom. They made me go to church my
whole childhood, get all the sacraments. I hated confession. Why did
I have to tell my secrets to a stranger who proceeded to scold me for
them? Like the time I told the priest my neighbor had asked to look
down my underpants the summer before I turned eleven, and since
I pulled them down myself I suspected it must have been my fault,
and the priest confirmed my suspicion.

Still, I *believed* back then. I'm not sure I could say the same for
my parents. They brought me to church because they thought they
were supposed to. And when my mother's father died, she stopped going altogether, didn't even go back to bargain with God when she was
diagnosed with cancer. So my dad and I bargained for her, and he continued to take me to church until I left for college. That first semester,
I often joined the other Catholic students at Mass in the quad. Right
before spring break, though, I stopped. Something happened that I
wanted to forget, something that damaged the part of me that believed, like a scratch in a record so I could no longer hear God's voice.

I stared at the empty corner where the BI6FOOT truck had
turned. "Yeah," I agreed with my dad, too late. "Funny."

❧

When I wasn't working with my dad, I went to parties. The party
spot was in a forest called Genevieve Jump. There's a legend attached

to the name, which goes like this: Some servant girl hundreds of years ago is chased by a group of prominent townsmen trying to rape her, and she runs into the woods to escape them. They follow, and she finds herself on the ledge of a cliff. Jump, Genevieve, Jump! they taunt, not thinking she will. But she does. And while the legend says that halfway down she turned into a bird, the truth is she probably just died, dashed on the rocks below. But at least she got a forest named after her.

The woods were dense and blue-green, the floor blanketed with pine and studded with moss-covered rocks, cut through with narrow trails leading to a clearing. That's where the parties happened. Someone would build a fire. Sometimes someone would bring a keg, but usually there was just a lot of booze in backpacks and coolers. Always there was someone playing guitar. Always there were faces I half-knew in the firelight.

That night, I got a text about a party and drove my dad's truck to the lot by the woods. As I was walking up the trail, I heard rustling. I stopped and turned toward the noise. I heard leaves crunching and then saw a dark shape, larger than myself, moving through the trees. My heart quickened; I thought of the BI6FOOT truck, the *I BELIEVE*. I heard another noise behind me then—it was a couple acquaintances from high school, walking up the trail carrying a cooler. I turned back to the shape in the woods, but it was running off, a streak of white. I shook my head, laughing at myself. A deer. That BI6FOOT truck was giving me ideas.

About a dozen other people were in the clearing. I sat on a log beside the couple I'd walked up with, and they offered me a beer. I declined. Over the past year at college, vodka had become my drink of choice, the best drink for forgetting.

I drank with these two, a girl and guy who'd been dating since high school, and we told sad stories: a kid none of us knew too well who'd died of an overdose, another who'd died in a motorcycle accident. When there was a pause in conversation and I had downed a quarter of my bottle and was feeling a glow, my mind went back to BI6FOOT.

"Have you guys heard of the Sasquatch Society?" I asked.

The guy laughed and rolled his eyes, and his girlfriend playfully hit him. "Shut up," she said. "My uncle's a member. He goes to the woods and tries to get photos. I think he's part of some alien hunter group too. People around here are into weird shit."

"Unemployment," the guy followed up. "Too much time on their hands."

I stood up, swayed, stared into the woods.

"Do you guys think he's out there?"

"My uncle?"

"No," I said. "Bigfoot."

"You're drunk."

I saw someone playing guitar on the other side of the fire, surrounded by a group of people, some I knew from high school, some who graduated ten or even twenty years ago. I walked over, wondering how they all ended up here. In high school, everyone talked about wanting to get out, but then somehow they all returned, kept showing up at parties like this one. I guess I was no exception.

In California, the woods were different. The trees—it's hard to imagine their enormity without seeing them. Like dinosaur thighs. And the smell was unlike any forest I'd been to. The sharp scent of pine mingled with earthy cedar and dank loam. There was magic in those woods, strange bugs and light that danced. When I walked around the ferns, I imagined fairies lived under their leaves. My hometown woods, though, had never seemed full of magic. Until now. Because now, I was starting to wonder if something was hiding, waiting for me to find it. I wasn't sure I believed just yet. More like the poster hanging in Mulder's office in the *X-Files* reruns I sometimes watched with my parents: *I want to believe.*

I drifted and swayed. At one point I got up and started dancing. Someone grabbed my hips, but I broke away. Then I heard rustling in the woods and wandered over to the edge of the clearing. I made out a sound, low, guttural. I clutched my bottle and walked into the darkness.

Something was moving up against a tree. When I got a few feet in, I felt my heart drop when I realized it wasn't Sasquatch I was seeing; it was a man, pushing a woman up against a tree trunk, kissing her, rubbing his hands over her body. One breast was exposed, bare nipple to the cool night. My own nipples hardened, arousal or fear, I wasn't sure.

I stepped back and was about to walk away, but I landed on a twig, and the man turned around. His face had a thick look about it. His eyes burned through the darkness as they stared at me. I was afraid he was going to yell or chase me, but instead he smiled.

Somehow, that was worse.

⸙

I met Asher in the darkroom at college, though I didn't see him at first, just smelled him. It smelled like someone had been jogging through a spice market, and I was attracted to that smell even before he stepped out of the shadows. He had been taking one of his photos out of a developing tray when I came in. He was a photography major, declared, I found out later. I admired that kind of firm decision. I loved photography too, but was still undecided.

After our first meeting, Asher invited me to his dorm, which smelled like him and was delightfully messy, the walls plastered with art. The next week he invited me to a photography exhibit, and then we were pretty much a couple. We went to parties together, because that's what freshmen did, though I always got so much drunker than him. Asher once told me he liked me better when I was sober, which made me secretly happy even though I acted offended at the time. Everyone else at college seemed to like me better when I was drunk. Asher, to my great surprise, seemed to like me the way I was.

Over winter break, I found myself missing him. When I got back, I told him I was ready. We spent that first night after winter break on his small, squeaky mattress, trying to have sex for the first time. It took a while, and when he was finally able to enter me, it hurt—a stinging pain, sharp and burning. In the days afterward, I took naked selfies and immediately deleted them, trying to see what he saw when he looked at me. But then I remembered he wasn't seeing me like this; he was on top of me in the dark, too close to see the whole of me.

On the nights I didn't spend with him, I touched myself, tried to give myself pleasure and succeeded, only to be too self-conscious to come when he was inside me. Still, I enjoyed it—the way he lit a candle, dangerous because it was prohibited in the dorms, and the music he streamed from his computer, always some echoic guitar and sad voice like Nick Drake, the glow of the screen illuminating his silhouette as he leaned over me and asked *Is this okay?*, and *Are you ready?*, and *Does this feel good?*. The answer, with him, was always yes.

Asher was about the same height as me, which hadn't been the case with my few boyfriends from in high school. It was exhilarating, really, to stand toe to toe with a man and be staring directly into his eyes. He had one hazel eye and one green, and black hair that curled down over the light brown skin of his face, the product of a Haitian mom and an Irish dad. He was sensitive about his height, but I never thought of him as short because he carried himself with such confidence, like the time he stood on a picnic table in the quad during a thunderstorm and did an impression of Prince singing "Purple Rain" to a crowd of drunk freshmen.

One of Asher's friends from photography class, a blond boy named Erit, was about a foot taller than him. Erit was his nickname, pronounced *Errit-Errit-Errit*; he said life was about making records, and he was scratching them. Erit was a senior and was a staple at all the parties, in dorms and frat houses and the ones in the quad that got busted, and he always had a new girl, usually a freshman.

One night there was a party in Erit's dorm. Asher left early; I stayed. There was music, dancing. Someone snorted a Xanax and fainted. We laughed. Erit touched my neck and told me it was small, so small he could probably snap it. Somehow, I took that as a compliment. Plastering the walls were posters of musicians and naked women, not the artistic black-and-white nudes that Asher had on his wall, but glaring, oil-slicked porn stars with impossibly pert breasts. I noticed these naked women more as the crowd thinned out and became just a few of us, and finally just me and Erit. By that point I was drifting in and out of blackout. I found myself sitting on the toilet, not sure how I got there. I was aware of my body only in long blinks of consciousness.

The next morning, I woke up to fuzzy light, dry mouth, pounding head, a sick feeling. I was in Erit's bed, naked. The significance of that didn't hit me until he said, his back turned, "You need to get the morning-after pill."

I tried to remember what happened but couldn't. The memory was in a locked drawer that I couldn't open, would never be able to open. I would never know if I wanted it or if I didn't. At first I didn't tell anyone, but I wanted answers to those questions, and I figured if I couldn't answer them, maybe someone else could. I told my roommate, then my RA. They both laughed it off: *That's what happens when you drink too much.* I told God, too, and he seemed to call the same thing down to me in his booming, deep voice, and then I began to wonder why God's voice was booming and deep, and not more like mine or my mother's. That's when I stopped going to Mass and swore off ever going to confession, convinced the priest would say the same thing, or worse, chastise me for having sex in the first place.

When I came home for spring break, my mother seemed concerned. Is everything all right, honey? I said yes. My dad sat me down and told me money was tight, and I would not be able to return to school in the fall. Even with my scholarship, tuition was expensive, and so was airfare. He told me this with a grave face, holding his body stiff. Okay, I shrugged. I won't go back.

I spent my final two months of college drinking as much as I could, trying to forget—but what was there to forget, exactly? I was waiting for someone to tell me I was wronged, but no one did. The only one I didn't tell was Asher. He texted and left voicemails and finally knocked on my door, asking me what was the matter, but after weeks of me ignoring him, he finally cooled, and since what we had was unstated anyway, there was no messy breakup. We just stopped hanging out. The day I left campus for the last time in May, I was hoping to say goodbye to Asher, but instead Erit caught me in the quad. He gave me a hug, and I hugged him back, even though his body made me feel like retreating into a shell. The last image I had of college was Erit's face, smiling, and then the feeling of his eyes on me as I walked away.

꘎

The morning after the party in the woods, my dad woke me and said we had to work, so I popped a couple Advil, gulped some coffee, and followed him out to the driveway. He stopped short.

"Why's the truck parked so crooked?"

The coffee churned in my stomach. "I was tired, I guess?" I looked down at my hands, tried scratching some of the dirt out from under my nails. "Sorry."

He stared at me for a long time like he wanted to say something. Finally he just said, "Let's go."

I hopped in the truck, and we drove to the church, a five-minute drive through town. We had just finished the roof, so we were moving on to the steeple. My dad said there were only minor repairs. We were going to replace some of the old siding and fix the little vented windows my dad called *louvers*, but it turned out, for a minor job, there was a lot of work involved. Rather than using a ladder, one of us had to be in a harness attached to a pulley, suspended in between the scaffold and the steeple. My dad set everything up, but when he tried to put on the harness, it wouldn't buckle over his beer-and-soda-swollen belly, even when he loosened the straps.

"What is this, made for kids?" he grumbled. "I bet that's why I got it so cheap."

I watched him struggle with the harness, his big hands fumbling with the buckle. Finally I said, "I can do it." I needed to do something to make up for drunk driving his truck the night before.

"No." He shook his head. "I'll just call Red or Flint." His buddies always had colorful names. He took out his phone.

"I want to do it, Dad."

"Are you sure?" he asked, and asked again like a hundred times as he attached the harness to me. Then, as I was being hoisted up, he switched to, "Are you okay?"

At first it was almost fun, like being a kid on the swings at a carnival, but as I got higher I began to feel unmoored. I wanted to grab hold of something, but there was nothing except the steeple, which I couldn't wrap my arms around. I swayed in the air, imagined myself falling like Genevieve Jump, dashed on the sidewalk. I thought about praying, but could no longer imagine who I'd be praying to. My heart was speeding, pounding against the harness, which was squeezing my chest, making it hard to breathe. Everything seemed brighter. The cars sped by below, so far away but so loud. A car horn blared and a man yelled something out the window at me, making my heart speed faster. I started to shake.

"I'm not okay," I squawked. And then, louder: "Get me down!"

My dad lowered me as fast as he could and let me sit in the grass still wearing the harness, crying. I knew he was looking at me, wondering what to do, feeling helpless, but I was neck-deep in the muck of my own feelings. Hungover, tired, and trembling, I didn't even know what I was saying. Later, when he drove me home, my dad told me that I kept repeating, "I wasn't sure, I wasn't sure."

⚘

I decided to take the next week off. My dad said the steeple was a bigger job than he'd thought, so he'd get a few of his buddies to help him. I also decided to take the week off from drinking. It was strange, waking up with a clear head. Every morning I got up early, took my camera, and drove my mom's car to the woods.

For the first few days, I stayed on the trails, breathing in pine, listening to birds. By mid-week, I was venturing off-trail, searching for something I wouldn't yet admit to myself. I was sure there was magic in these woods, even though we were minutes from a highway. By the end of the week, I had photos of trees, birds, leaves, dappled light, mossy rocks, my own shadow—and nothing else.

Then, on Friday, after wandering the woods all morning, I walked back to the lot and saw the BI6FOOT truck. The driver must have been searching for the same thing I was. I went back to the car and called my mom, asked her if it was okay if I kept her car out a bit longer. She said it was fine. She was a kindergarten teacher and was off for the summer, spent her days dipping her feet in the same plastic kiddie pool I used to splash in over a decade ago, her chest flattened under her bathing suit from the mastectomy, a sight that made my knees weak but also made me want to be strong like her. I was about to end the call, but on the other end of the line there was a long pause thick with some kind of question.

"Honey, is something wrong?"

I wanted to tell her. I wanted so badly to tell her what was wrong, but I couldn't. So instead, I talked about Bigfoot.

"You know that truck I was telling you about, with all the Bigfoot stickers? It's here. So I'm gonna wait 'til the driver gets back, maybe see if they're heading over to one of those Sasquatch meetings."

I could hear the worry lines forming on her forehead. But all she said was, "Just be careful. And be home for dinner, okay?"

I was oddly disappointed when I hung up. Maybe part of me wanted her to give voice to her worries, to confirm what I was beginning to suspect about the world. I slumped down in the seat, waiting for the BI6FOOT driver to return. It took over an hour, but he finally did, a man wearing a baseball cap that shadowed his face and holding what looked, in my first heart-pounding glance, like a gun, but was actually a camera with a very long lens. When the truck pulled out of the lot, I did, too, and I followed it down the road into town. We drove past the church, where I saw my dad's friend Flint poised in the air, dangling beside the steeple. He was laughing, smoking a cigarette up there, making it look so easy.

The truck pulled into the Elk Lodge lot. I parked on the far end and watched the man emerge from the truck. I waited until he had entered the building to get out of my car. I was in luck: there was a flyer at the door advertising the Sasquatch Society.

When I entered the large hall, I felt eyes on me. I was suddenly too aware of my body. I waved awkwardly, but no one waved back, just resumed their coffee and conversation. The chairs were arranged in a semi-circle like an AA meeting or a therapy group, both of which I had attended very briefly and then dropped in my first couple weeks home from college. I couldn't tell which man was the BI6FOOT driver, because everyone in the room looked alike, late-middle-aged white men wearing work boots with relatively little evidence of work. There were variations, of course; some had bushy beards, some had scruff; some shirts were emblazoned with Budweiser logos, some with American flags, some with both. They all stood with their legs spread, large men with beer bellies in various stages of gestation, their voices competing for loudness.

I hovered near the refreshment table until most of the men were sitting down, and then I grabbed a powdered donut and sat down, too. I shifted in my seat, pulling at the hem of my shorts. A man stood at the front next to a screen and welcomed everyone to the meeting. I thought he would launch into the slideshow, but instead he pointed at me.

"It looks like we have a new member."

Everyone stared. I tried to smile. "Hi," I croaked, powder from the donut stuck in my throat. They examined me for another excruciating moment, as if waiting for me to share something like in the therapy group, but I was as wordless now as I was then. They turned back to the slideshow.

The man up front clicked through slide after slide of fuzzy pictures, the men claiming they saw something at the edges, a snatch of fur, a shadow. I began to find the way they were talking about Bigfoot unpleasant, their voices dripping with hunger. *Caught*, they said. *Caught a glimpse. Caught a scent. Caught on camera.* One man stood up and shared his encounter story. He said he rode his motorcycle out to Genevieve Jump in the middle of the night and walked

through the woods, off-trail, no flashlight, nothing. He followed every footstep, and eventually he felt his skin brushed by the rough
fur of some large beast. He tried to grab hold of it, but the creature
growled and ran away. He knew it was Bigfoot because it had a smell
like nothing else. A deep musk, more pungent than a herd of deer,
like the smell of a wet hairy pussy.

The men laughed. I stiffened.

The speaker looked at me, as if suddenly remembering I was
there. "Oh. Sorry, sweetie." They laughed again.

I had an urge to flee but decided to wait until the slideshow
ended. Before I could leave, though, one of the men cornered me by
the donuts.

"So you're interested in Bigfoot, huh?"

I nodded, tried not to look him in the eye. "I guess so."

He chuckled. "We don't get many girls here." He paused, stepped
closer, trying to be conspiratorial. "Don't worry, I'll protect you."

I could smell his breath. Coffee and gingivitis. The fluorescent
lights were bright, and everyone around me was moving, voices in
the background like mechanical chirping. Without saying anything,
I shrank away from the man and ran out of the building. I sat in the
car and cried.

Next to the lot was a playground with rusty equipment I used
to play on after school. The empty swings creaked in the wind and
seemed to taunt me: *How could you have believed?* I thought about
going home but didn't want to face my parents and their worried
foreheads, their unasked questions, the answers to those questions
swarming inside me, stinging. I needed something to ease the sting.
So I went back to the woods.

❧

That night, I walked the trail until I heard the pop and crackle of the bonfire, the faint music of bottles clinking, sloppy guitar strumming. In the clearing, I saw about a dozen people. I recognized them as regulars, but at the moment they felt like strangers. I sat on a log alone and drank until I didn't feel alone anymore.

I got up and danced with a red-headed girl I knew from high school. I chugged gulps of vodka until the woods spun around me even when I wasn't spinning. Eventually the faces at the party blended together, but there was one that stood out. It was the man with the thick face I had seen a week ago pushing a girl up against a tree. The whites of his eyes were red. He smiled and asked my friend to kiss me. She did, and I let her. Then the man took my hand, and I followed him, one foot in front of the other, into the woods.

I tripped and fell onto the damp leaves. The man rolled me over onto my back.

"Oopsie daisy," he said, looking down at me. He was so tall, a skyscraper. I felt dizzy even lying on the ground. I hoped he would help me up, but instead he bent over me. I made a feeble attempt to rise.

"Where you going?" he asked softly, and began to kiss my neck.

I felt vomit rising in my throat. He unzipped my hoodie and ran his hands over my breasts. Finally I pushed against his chest, and when I couldn't shove him off, I raised one of my legs and kneed him as hard as I could in his groin. He rolled off me, and I ran.

I didn't know where I was running. I was deep in the woods before I realized I was lost. I wanted to lie down. And then I heard something. A rustling that sounded like the swish of chiffon skirts. Twigs snapping like wishbones. And I smelled musk, deep and dusky, reminding me of old churches and the basements of childhood duplexes, reminding me of menstrual blood or the scent left on my fingers after I touched myself at night thinking of Asher. I thought of

Asher now. I thought of Erit. Then I thought of the thick-faced man. Had he followed me?

But it was not him.

I saw the shape as it passed. Even in the dark I could tell it was not human, nor was it animal. It was something else entirely.

I always thought Bigfoot would have a lumbering frame, eight feet tall, five hundred pounds. But this creature was lithe. It wove through the trees gracefully, effortlessly, while I followed, clumsy and drunk.

The woods became less dense, and finally there was a clearing, and on the other end of the clearing, a cave. As the figure approached the cave, I was able to get a better look at it, the light of the half moon shining down. Rust-brown fur over the body. Slightly bigger than a human man, but not by much. And a shape that curved outward at the hips, a shape sort of like my mother's. This creature: it had breasts. She turned to stretch in the moonlight, made a whining growl, a sound of pleasure.

Bigfoot was female.

My fear, which had followed me here, was gone. I stepped closer to the lip of the clearing. I tried to step quietly to avoid detection, but the truth was I wanted her to notice me. I was so alone. I wanted this creature to see me, to know me. She was alone, too.

I stared at her, willing her to stare back. Finally, she did. First it was a head-cocked empty stare in my direction, and then her gaze narrowed, focused, and the darkness of her eyes seemed to capture me in a beam of their light. I wondered how she saw me. Small figure, dressed in black, long hair wild with twigs, I may have appeared to her a kindred spirit. I was, I wanted to tell her. I wanted to tell her so many things. But the way she looked at me, the kindness softening her eyes, it seemed like she could smell it on me, in the knowing way that animals do, like a wound. Maybe she was wounded too.

She turned and walked into the cave. Heart pounding, I followed. But when I entered, there was no sign of her. The only thing that remained was her musk. She must have escaped deeper into the darkness, where I wouldn't follow. I stared into that darkness for a long time, hoping to see her shape, until fatigue took over and I reclined on the cool cave floor. I was asleep in minutes. I may have been dreaming, but I thought I felt my cheek brushed with fur, coarse and warm. I thought I felt arms carry me to softer ground.

❆

When I woke, I was lying on a pile of leaves. I didn't see any sign of Bigfoot. I walked out of the cave, and in the weak dawn light I was able to find my way back to the trail. I followed it down to the parking lot, where my car was the only one left, and then I drove through the summer morning, cool enough to be misty but with the threat that heat would soon settle in. As I drove down the forest-framed highway, I kept wondering if I'd see a dark shape standing on the side of the road, staring at me as I drove away. I didn't.

In town, I approached the corner of the church. The work was almost done now. I pulled over and got out of the car. I thought about the many people who had worked on the church over its three hundred years, from the ones who built it to those, like us, who repaired it, the evidence of our hands invisible. Deep magenta slashed across the sky behind the steeple. I had missed this when I was away at college, looking up at steeples, at points converging in the sky, evidence of our blind human reach into mystery like the faith of a girl leaping off a cliff and believing she'll fly. The church looked fresh and young, new again, paint unchipped, smooth and white like spilled milk, but a scaffold was still erected beside it, a sign of repairs unfinished. A small bird perched atop the steeple cocked its head, as if asking me a question. I stood there a long time searching for the answer.

A truck pulled up to the curb behind me. When I turned, I saw my mom and dad rushing toward me, their faces knotted with concern. They stood on either side of me, a thousand unsaid words swarming, and because I didn't know how to say sorry, I pointed at the bird.

"Starling, I think," my dad said after a while. "Shakespeare's bird."

"Up close," my mom said, "they're iridescent. Green, purple." She picked a leaf out of my hair. "They're actually quite beautiful."

The bird cocked its head again, and this time I knew the answer to its question. I held out my hands, palms up, between my mom and dad, like I used to do when I was little and asked to be lifted into the air. They grabbed hold.

"I have something to tell you," I said, "and I hope you'll believe."

THE HALL OF HUMAN ORIGINS

THERE WAS A RHYME we schoolgirls repeated in the years before we went through Placement: *Slats are fat / Gins are thin.* Even then, before we knew what a Slat was, we knew we didn't want to be one. And while the rhyme as a whole wasn't true, we did sometimes catch glimpses of the Slats on our rare field trips to the city, and whether they were fat or thin or in between, none of them looked healthy, alive. The thin ones were gray and sallow and hollow-eyed, while the fat ones were corpulent, elephant skin lacing the backs of their necks, and everyone in between had red sores on their arms, black spots in their mouths where their teeth used to be, showing them off when they smiled at us as we rode past in a pink school bus on our way to The Museum of Modern Man. Because of the missing teeth, their smiles looked menacing, but sometimes I could swear I caught a glimpse of yearning in those smiles, something desperate to show itself as kind. When the buses passed, the Slats watched, their wild eyes following us, searching each small window for our faces. I didn't like to think about it much, but sometimes I remembered it was possible that those women could have been our mothers. One of them could have even been my mother. She could have been searching the bus windows for me.

❧

"Which one do you think you'll choose?" My roommate, Rebecca, was dangling her long bare legs over the side of our bunk. She'd asked me this same question almost every night for the last two weeks, as we neared Placement. Each time, my answer was the same: "I don't know. Haven't thought about it."

The first part was true: I didn't know. But I *had* been thinking about it, a lot. At night while Rebecca snored lightly above me. In the communal baths, where the Nans instructed us to scrub every inch of our bodies. On our weekly nature walks to get a dose of green. And during classes, where we were taught all the skills we might need depending on where we were Placed: how to sew, how to cook, how to iron men's clothes, how to care for an infant, how to teach, how to dispense basic first aid, how to guide a woman through birth, how to lie down when someone tells you to lie down, how to say yes even if you mean no, how to give a proper blow job. We practiced on bananas.

Rebecca growled in frustration. "You're such a liar!" She threw a pillow at me, and I caught it and hugged it to my chest. It smelled like her: floral shampoo, the oil of her scalp, the cheap perfume she bought from the commissary with the meager allowance we received from doing our weekly chores.

The school had given us five choices: Gin, Nan, Blue, Cow, or Slat. While we were allowed to state our preference, our teachers warned us we wouldn't always get our first choice; it depended on the results of our Placement Exam. They assured us, though, if we worked hard, we would be happy with our placement. The majority of the girls chose Gin because somehow we knew it was the best choice, even if we didn't even know what the word stood for. We were only just now, a few weeks before our Placement Exam, beginning to be told what each of the names meant and what their roles were. We knew, though, to be a Slat was the worst. We knew this because they looked so sad, so desperate, so unhealthy. We knew because we saw them on the streets. The others weren't as visible to us, except the Nans, who were our teachers, our nannies, our nurses.

"I've always wanted to be a Gin," Rebecca said. "Why don't you just choose that like the rest of us?" Her toenails were painted a forbidden Fire-Engine Red. We'd painted them in secret a few days prior, but I'd scraped mine off the next day, too afraid of getting caught. The only approved color for toenails was Eggshell Pink.

I shrugged, unable to articulate my concerns. What did a Gin even do? All we were told was that Gins married rich dudes, got to live in fancy houses, got someone to take care of the cleaning. That sounded good—who wants to do their own cleaning?—but it seemed suspicious somehow, like there was something ugly hiding under all that pretty, like a cracked yellow nail under pink polish.

⚶

The teacher was going through a slideshow, repeating a rhyme, which is how so much of our learning was conveyed to us, even now, well into our teens. *Oh, the things that you can do / when you choose to be a Blue.* There were pictures of smiling women cleaning toilets, working at an assembly line, packing boxes, picking up trash, painting houses, working cash registers, stocking shelves, delivering packages. Rebecca, beside me, groaned and rolled her eyes. "Who the hell smiles while they plunge a toilet?"

The teacher snapped the lights on. "What was that, Rebecca?"

Rebecca turned red. "Nothing." She stifled a giggle and squeezed my hand, and I felt a lightning bolt of pleasure rush through my whole body.

Next, the teacher clicked through a slideshow about the Cows. *Everybody will say Wow / when you choose to be a Cow.* We already had a pretty good idea what they did: pushed out babies, fed them with their big udders. We sometimes mocked them, made mooing noises and called them Breeders, but at night I'm sure we all longed for a mother, the closeness against another's body, the umbilical connection. I know I did.

None of us really knew where we came from. We might have come from a Cow who'd had too many children to keep, or we might have been snatched from a Slat, who were not allowed to keep any children they bore. It was highly unlikely our mothers were Gins or Nans, as these women were not allowed to get pregnant, though we were never told the exact mechanism that kept this from happening. It's possible a Blue family might have given us up. Along with the Cows, Blues were the only women who were allowed to have and keep children, one of the selling points our teachers drilled into us. As a Blue, you could have your own children, as many as you could conceive with as many men as you wanted, and you could live with your kids in a small ramshackle house on the edge of the city. All you had to do was work seventy-five hours a week at a factory with no breaks, which meant most of these children languished alone in their shacks all day, eating scraps like dogs, sitting in their own filth, until they grew old enough to join the ranks of the Blues or the Slats or until they migrated to the city, where they sat on the streets begging for crust from fancy restaurants where well-manicured Gins sat primly across from the too-white smiles of their sleek-suited husbands. Surely sometimes a kind-hearted Blue mother, realizing she could not care for her children, would drop her daughters here, at this large brick compound just outside the city, a finishing school that promised to raise girls into women and prepare them for whatever role they chose.

That is what this place promised: choice. And hope. I wondered how many desperate Blues walked their daughters miles to reach the gate of the compound with a dream that they were providing their children with a better life than they'd had, or at least a chance at it. I wondered, too, if those dreams ever actually came true.

※

Rebecca's exam was the day before mine. Despite her seeming confidence, I could tell she was nervous because she was sleeping fitfully, tossing and turning above me all night, her mattress groaning. She was gone by the time I got up, the scent of her shampoo hanging in the room like an invisible garden. I'd known that smell for ten years now, as that's how long we'd been roommates, since we left the nursery at six years old.

When I caught up with her in the quad during free time, she was beaming.

"I got it," she said. "I'm a Gin!"

I felt the lightning bolt again, but this time it was painful, and the pain intensified when she told me she was leaving tomorrow.

"That's when I'm meeting him," she said. "My husband."

She was smiling what seemed to be a genuine smile. I tried to do the same, but it probably looked more like a grimace. "Do you even, like, know anything about him?"

She shrugged. "They said he's very successful." She paused, and I could see something start to cloud over in her eyes, but they quickly cleared. "I'll have my own house, you know. When you're settled, you can come over. Like for tea or some shit." She laughed, put her arm around me. "That's why I want you to be a Gin. We can hang out more that way."

That was reason enough for me. "I'll try," I promised.

※

The next morning I woke early for my exam. Rebecca was still sleeping; she had packed all her belongings into a small suitcase the previous night and would be leaving by noon, before I even returned from my exam. I wanted to say goodbye to her, but I didn't feel right waking her up. So I stared at her sleeping face for a long time, whispering everything I'd always wanted to tell her, wishing her luck, telling her I'd miss her and I hoped to see her again. As I was walking out of the room, I thought I heard her say, "Goodbye." Maybe she had been pretending to sleep and had heard everything. I carried that sweet thought with me to my exam.

The first part of the exam was easy. There were about a hundred multiple choice questions that quizzed us on reading, writing, arithmetic, science, and history, in addition to rules of law, social customs, gender roles, grooming, childcare, housework, and sex acts. There was a section that asked us to rank the Placements according to our preference. I put Gin first, and then Nan, Blue, Cow, and Slat, in that order. I wasn't sure of any of it, except that I'd be happy if I was able to continue seeing Rebecca.

The next part of the exam was more uncomfortable. One of the Nans performed a physical exam, including a gynecological one, and a male photographer took a picture of my naked body. The Nans had told us to expect it, but still, I felt vulnerable and cold standing there completely naked in front of the wall, not knowing what to do with my hands. The Nan who examined me, at least, was very gentle, ginger even, using the smallest of baby speculums, barely the size of her pinky.

After it was all over, I had to wait for two hours outside the room while they conferred and graded my exam. Strange men walked in and out, each of them looking me up and down before they entered.

As I waited in the hallway, I stared out the window, hoping to catch a glance of Rebecca leaving. When I did see her, she was too far away for me to wave. She put her suitcase into a black car. The Nan who had walked her there gave her a hug, and then Rebecca got in the car and was gone. I closed my eyes and willed myself into the body of that Nan, wanting to feel Rebecca's warmth one last time, wanting to give her strength for the life ahead of her, a life that would probably be lived without me.

But maybe it wouldn't be. The Nan who had examined me came out of the room and, with a smile on her face, told me that I qualified to be a Gin. I was shocked. She continued talking, about the man I'd marry and when I'd leave, but I wasn't really listening. All I could think of was that I'd still be able to see Rebecca. I imagined us meeting up after our husbands went to work, having brunch in our big houses, having tea in our big gardens, and then driving into the big city to visit all the big museums, and entering all the halls previously restricted to us, seeing all the exhibits we'd never seen.

＊

To my disappointment, my departure was delayed. I spent my days alone in the dorm room, the top bunk stripped of linens, cold and alien and lonely. One by one, my few other friends left too. I couldn't believe my luck in becoming a Gin, because so many of these other girls ended up as Blues, Cows, Nans. I hadn't heard of anyone becoming a Slat, though, and I began to wonder exactly what one had to do to earn that Placement, how bad one had to be.

The dorm was emptying out. We were on the fourth floor, in the east wing, and the medical unit was in the west wing. The day before I was meant to leave, I wandered into the west wing, which we were normally forbidden from entering. I was hoping to see some exciting medical emergency, or maybe witness one of the Cows giving birth. Instead, I saw Rebecca. They were wheeling her on a gurney from one room into another. She wore a surgical cap and gown, and her body was covered in a paper sheet. I ran to her—she was not injured, just groggy from anesthesia. The nurse wheeling her gave me a sharp look and told me sternly I was not allowed there.

"What happened?" I asked. "Are you okay?"

Rebecca shook her head, and a tear slipped out the corner of one eye. The nurse was trying to push me away now, calling for the orderlies.

"They sewed me back up!" Rebecca cried. "He tore me, and they sewed me up. He said they're making me tight again." She began sobbing and grabbed my wrist. "What if they do it every time?"

An orderly pried Rebecca's hand off me and pulled me away while the nurse wheeled the gurney down the hall. I wasn't sure, but I thought I could hear Rebecca calling after me. It sounded like *Run away*.

ઝ

As I lay in bed that night, the cold fear inside me grew so big that it threatened to separate me from my own body, and I had to run to keep up with it. I gathered some clothes from my drawers and shoved them in a bag. I grabbed a couple old granola bars and stuffed those in too. I was running out of time—the Nans would be coming around soon for midnight room checks—but I searched my desk for the notes that Rebecca and I had passed in class over the years, and when I found them I gingerly dropped those in my bag. I thought I might need something to remember her by.

Getting out was easy enough. Everyone was asleep. There was some activity down the corridor in the west wing, but they didn't notice me. When I got outside, I slipped onto the oak-dotted quad, walking quickly rather than running because running might attract more attention. Ahead of me was the forest, the stand of trees that led into the deeper woods, which, I remembered from our weekly walks, opened up to a highway on the other side. Was there a fence? I couldn't remember now. I hopped into a jog, my backpack jostling behind me, my breath forming clouds in front of me. And then I saw a light.

A small yellow square, a reflection on the grass. I turned around, and maybe that was my mistake. In a third-floor window, I saw one of the Nans staring down at me, the same one who had examined me so gently last week, her fingers probing my labia, trying not to hurt me. I realized now the care she had taken was not for me, but for my future husband.

Well. Fuck that.

I ran. I ran as fast as I could into those woods, finding the trail and following it all the way to the fence. I heard commotion behind me and knew that the Nan must have alerted the guards. I turned around and saw the first of them starting toward me, his hands out, telling me to remain still. It seemed like he was afraid of me, as if I had a gun or something.

I turned back to the fence. It was high, but I was sure I could scale it. I had one thing these people didn't: I was young. I trusted my body. And for the first time I realized how much I cherished it, my body, and how important it was that it stay mine. I grabbed the fence.

Next thing I knew I was on the ground, a burning smell around me and the shock of a thousand bees buzzing through my body. The guard and the Nan from the window stood over me, looking sympathetic. I wanted to ask what happened but couldn't seem to open my mouth. They knew what I was asking, though.

"It's electrified, honey. You never had a chance."

❧

I slept hard that night, and when I bolted up in bed the next morning, I saw a Nan standing in the doorway. She turned her back and explained my fate as I got dressed clumsily, the skin of my hand bandaged, my body still electric and achy. I would no longer be a Gin. I sighed in relief, nearly crying.

"You'll be a Slat," she said, turning around to face me. "I don't take pleasure in telling you this."

I sat down on my bed, letting the idea sink in. Slat? I'd have to live on the streets, among those ugly women. I looked at myself in the mirror. I couldn't be a Slat. I was too young. I said so to the Nan.

"They were all young once," she replied. There may have been a hint of sadness in her voice, but it was fleeting. She clapped her hands together. "Now gather your things. The car is waiting to take you to the city."

I couldn't move. I just stared at my face in the mirror and imagined myself with no teeth, sunken cheeks, imagined my body being used every night by a different man, imagined sleeping next to those other women, their diseased breath seeping into me. I cried. I pled with the Nan, make me anything else, make me a Blue, a Cow, make me one of you. At least give me a bed to sleep in. A body to call my own.

She held me for a moment as I sobbed, and then offered me a single tissue. She handed me my bag, conveniently packed last night. At least I still had Rebecca's notes.

As the car drove me away, I watched the buildings of the compound in which I'd grown up recede into the distance for the last time, getting smaller and smaller until they looked like little castles out of a picture book, and I could almost imagine nothing bad ever happened there. The woods whipped by me, and then the houses of the big men with their Gin wives, and then the smaller shacks that belonged to the Blues, and then the gray buildings of the city rose up in front of me. We crossed a bridge, and I knew that my old life was over.

The man driving the car stopped beside a long alleyway, where a throng of women mingled, stretching their bodies like dancers in preparation for the night's work, holding slim beer bottles with their thick hands, changing clothes like actresses between acts, washing their dirty underthings in even dirtier buckets.

"Here's where you get out," the driver said. I pleaded with him to keep driving, to take me away and find me somewhere else to go. I offered him favors, a blow job, my virginity, but he ignored me, rolled up the window between the back seat and the front, and then pressed a button that opened my door. I got out.

I stood at the entrance of the alleyway, afraid of these women whom I'd only ever seen from a distance. They stopped what they were doing for a moment and stared at me, their eyes softening with each passing second until they seemed liquid, like the eyes of a puppy or a doe. And then I didn't notice their missing teeth because I was looking only at their soft eyes, and I didn't notice the elephant skin or the red marks because I saw only their soft arms opening up as they walked toward me, ready to embrace me, to welcome me, to take me into their fold, and all of them called me baby and held my head as I cried.

❦

I'm not sure how many years I spent as a Slat before I finally saw Rebecca again. It felt like forever, but I still had some teeth— most of my molars, some of my upper, both canines—so it must not have been that long. We normally slept during the day so we could be awake all night, our busiest hours. But when business was slow, or anytime we were low on money or food, we'd keep ourselves up through the morning and afternoon to go begging. We'd hover out-side fancy brunch places, grabbing leftover quiche off the outdoor tables before the waitress cleared them away, or we'd sit next to the wrought-iron fence that separated the restaurant patio from the sidewalk, waiting for some sympathetic Gin to drop coins or baguette or mints into our opened guitar case. We didn't own a guitar, but somehow we'd gotten ahold of this case, and anytime I carried it around I felt special, as if I could make music, and once in a while if I carried it just the right way walking with just the right rhythm, the coins and mints rattling inside the empty case did become a certain type of song.

I was sitting outside a restaurant with the other Slats when I saw her. She sat down at a table near the fence. A tall man was with her, her husband, his slicked-back silver hair glaring against the sun. He was wearing brown loafers and khaki shorts, and his calf muscles were tanned and incredibly defined. I didn't look at his face. And Rebecca, I almost didn't recognize her at first. Had she grown taller, or was it my feeling of having shrunk? Her hair was bobbed and dyed platinum, and she was wearing a slim-fitting white dress with black piping, something worn by rich women in their thirties, which was, I realized, what she was now. When she turned to look at us, I saw that her face was still beautiful, but there was a touch of sadness to her plump mouth, the mouth I had always wanted to kiss, and her eyes had lost their spark of mischief, replaced by a dead, mascara-framed gaze. I wanted to hug her, to shake her, to ask if she remembered me.

But it seemed she didn't. She looked away from us and back at her husband, who was ordering Prosecco. I inched closer so I was flush against the fence. I wanted to hear their conversation. But they sat in silence as they waited for their drinks and then their food, the husband on his phone, Rebecca stealing glances at us and then looking down at the charcuterie board as if she were trying to figure out the formula for an impossibly hard math problem. And then she stared directly at me through the bars of the fence, and she seemed to figure out the answer.

We stared into each other's eyes for the longest time that we ever had in all our years of knowing one another. As the moments wore on, I felt tears welling in my eyes, and I could see them shining in hers, too, until her husband snapped his fingers in front of her face and asked why she wasn't eating, what she was looking at. He followed her gaze, and even though we'd been sitting there the whole time, it was as if we'd suddenly materialized to him, and his expression wrinkled in disgust.

He called over the waitress, then the manager. This happened to us all the time, getting kicked out, but this was the first time I was being torn away from Rebecca, my best friend, my past. The manager asked us to leave, and while his voice was not impolite, it felt like a punch in the gut. I clung to the bars until my sisters pulled me away. Rebecca held my stare until her husband grabbed her jaw and roughed it back in his direction. In her eyes, I didn't see pity as I'd expected. I saw wistfulness and shame and desperation. I wondered if she saw the same in my eyes. I wondered if her shame, her desperation was greater than mine. After all, she had only her husband. I, at least, had these sisters.

Without me telling them anything, my sisters comforted me. They held me, rubbed my back, promised to take my clients so I could have the night all to myself, my body my own. I needed something to occupy my mind, to help me forget what I'd lost, so I did what we Slats sometimes did on our nights off: I sneaked into a museum. We had an arrangement with the night watchmen at several museums; in exchange for regular favors, they would leave the back doors unlocked. The newest arrangement was with the Museum of Natural History. Rebecca and I had always wanted to go here, but this was not one of the museums we schoolgirls were allowed to visit. It was from Before.

It was dark when I walked in, and my footsteps echoed in the atrium, accompaniment to the loneliness I'd been feeling. The exhibits were so dizzying they made me forget myself. I wandered drunk, unaware of time, letting images pass before me like a dreamscape: brown bears standing like large shadowy men, dinosaur skeletons and prehistoric beasts, planets and meteorites and so many creatures that seemed pulled from a fantastic picture book. In the Hall of North American Forests, I was overwhelmed with the feeling that I was walking through a magical place, and I found myself missing trees. Our schoolyard had been surrounded by them, the one beauty of that place besides Rebecca. The city streets, however, were only sparsely lined with imitation trees, which cleaned the air but were unliving, soulless. I stood in front of the Giant Sequoia. 1,400 years old. It was hard to fathom that much time. Older than my mother, whoever she was, my mother's mother, and her mother's mother, and so on back over a thousand years. It made me feel small and fragile, a gnat, a mote, myself an unnamed ancestor of some future descendant who I desperately hoped would have a future brighter than mine.

Eventually I wandered into the Hall of Human Origins, an exhibit called "Meet Your Relatives." Across the room, I saw a humanoid face shining through the darkness, and I jumped, my mind wheeling. Which Slat sister had sneaked in with me? Had Rebecca followed me here? Had I wandered into a dream world where I would be reunited with my family, where the mother I was taken from found her way back to me, or the child that had been ripped from my arms returned to me all grown up?

But, no. It was just Lucy, early hominid. I approached her shyly and examined the representation of her face glowing in the darkness beside her three-million-year-old bones. Though the bones showed that she was short as a child, she looked motherly to me, so I stood in front of her for a long time, imagining she was my mother and telling her everything. I told her the story of my life. I told her about Rebecca, and I promised that I would find her again or die trying. I told her that if I did die trying, I hoped someday someone would find my bones too, even if it were thousands or millions of years from now, and I hoped they'd give me a name and piece me back together until they could read my story in my bones: the bend in my ulna from when that man broke my arm, the spread in my hips from childbirth, the ache in my marrow when the infant was taken away, the grace in the bones of my feet that could once run so fast, the delicacy of my phalanges that applied makeup to my sisters' faces and wrote letters to Rebecca that she would never read, that would survive us both. Someday, I told Lucy, someday someone would remember us.

WILDER FAMILY

MANY YEARS LATER, WHEN she had reached old age, the woman would remember this as the pivotal moment—not what came after, not the life-transforming event of childbirth or its soul-molding aftermath—but this moment, this quick look down as she was driving home at dusk after picking up a pizza to bring home to her new husband for dinner, this split second she took her eyes off the road to glance at something inconsequential on her phone, this one careless moment in a lifetime of careful moments, the moment when a deer leapt, filled with the vigor and joy of life, directly in front of her car. She saw the blur of its body as she looked up, too late. There was a violent thud, and her head jerked forward as she slammed the brakes. She heard herself screaming, *Fuck!* And then there was stillness, quiet, a vacuum in which she expected herself to cry but no tears came, and she felt guilty for not crying. She had just killed something. She, who took spiders out of their apartment, dangled by one leg. She, who hopped over ants on the sidewalk, had felled this living creature.

The woman pulled over and got out of the car. One of her headlights was busted, but in the weak glare of the remaining one she could see the deer, who had made it to the other side of the road and lay there now, shuddering. The woman was cold, filled with dread of what she knew she had to do. She had to go to the deer, stare into its eyes, and look at what she'd done. And if it didn't expire, she'd have to call someone to put a bullet between those eyes.

But that wouldn't be necessary. By the time the woman crossed the road and got to the deer, it was still. The eyes stared, not yet empty, so the woman put her hand on the deer's neck, a place where it wasn't bloody and mangled, and looked into those eyes to avoid seeing the rest of its damaged body. She didn't want it to be alone when it passed, although she knew ultimately everyone, animal or human, was. She felt the warm pulsing in its neck grow weaker and weaker with each heartbeat, and then it stopped completely, and the eyes grew glassy and black, reflecting the starless sky.

The woman stayed in that position even after the deer died, and then her other senses opened up and she could smell the blood, the feces, the particular musk an animal emits when terrified, when dying. She heard a song from a nearby house. It was the night before Thanksgiving, and they were already playing Christmas music. *Sleep in heavenly peace. Sleep in heavenly peace.*

⁂

The next night, the woman decided she couldn't eat the turkey. I think I'm a vegetarian now? She phrased it like a question, but she was certain: she would no longer eat animal flesh. It was something she had toyed with for years, but since no one around her was vegetarian, and their small Midwestern town held limited options for vegetarian cuisine, she had never committed to it, not until now.

They were eating dinner with her husband's parents. They gave her a strange look when she refused the turkey. They were a meat-and-potatoes family, but they were also accepting of their only son's new wife, so they served her a plate of sides and went on with the meal. About halfway through, the woman excused herself to go to the bathroom. She felt a pain in her lower abdomen, similar to menstrual pain, but she knew her period wasn't due for a couple weeks. When she checked, her underwear was free of blood, so she took a few deep breaths, let the pain pass, and rejoined the family at the table.

Two weeks later, though, her period didn't come. She made an appointment with her gynecologist. She was worried—not about pregnancy, no, not about that. She had leukemia as a child, and the chemotherapy, she had been told, greatly reduced her chances of ever getting pregnant. But her mother had died young of ovarian cancer, and the woman was certain the pain she had experienced on Thanksgiving meant something sinister.

So when the doctor told her that she was perfectly healthy—and perfectly pregnant—the shock that ran through the woman seemed to block out everything else, even joy. She drove home trying to register the news, that new life was growing inside her, something she never thought could happen. She remembered the last time she and her husband had had sex, the night she hit the deer. She thought of the deer now. She pictured its shuddering body, the black eyes, the spark that left those eyes when it finally died. What was that spark, and where did it go? The woman had taken it; she had caused the death of another creature, and now she was being rewarded with this gift of new life. It didn't seem right at all.

❧

The heartbeat. Hearing it for the first time was the most magical moment in the woman's life. It echoed in the room, muffled and fuzzy, like a transmission from underwater. This second heartbeat, coming from deep inside her, from a creature the size of…what now? A pomegranate aril? She had signed up for a weekly email that compared the baby's development to various foods, mostly fruit. It was a bit odd, especially because the woman worked in the produce section of the supermarket. Every time she took out a box of plums or oranges or mangoes, she thought of the baby growing inside her, a sticky thing, a sweet thing, easily bruised, perishable.

The doctor frowned but quickly moved to a neutral face. What's wrong? the woman asked. Your baby's heart rate is just a little faster than normal, the doctor said. Nothing to be worried about.

The woman's husband patted her shoulder. Hearing the child's heartbeat seemed to soften him. When she had told him about the pregnancy initially, he had been angry, as if she had tricked him into something. You said you couldn't get pregnant! He had stalked off and spent the night in the spare room, but by morning he had apologized. I'm just scared, he'd said. Neither of them made much money. Who knew if she'd be able to go back to work after the baby? Childcare was expensive. Still, he told her then that he was happy about it, but he hadn't smiled until this moment, hearing the baby's heartbeat in the small white room, the stocking-legged doctor standing beside them.

He reassured her now, echoing the doctor's words. Nothing to be worried about. They could see her knitting her brows together. She never could hide her fear; it manifested itself all over her body. She nodded, clenching her fists.

⁂

The months wore on. The woman continued working in the produce department, avoiding as best she could the areas of the store with offending smells. Passing by the meat department, she felt a blinding hatred. Several times she had thrown up from the smell. Miraculously, the nausea lifted sometime in late winter, and then in spring there were glorious months where she felt completely normal, back to her old self in spite of her growing abdomen. She ate every-thing she could get her hands on, except meat.

As spring melted into summer, new aches and pains came: shoot-ing sciatica pains; carpal tunnel pains in her wrists; ankle pains from carrying so much extra weight; itchy skin where the stretch marks bloomed on her lower abdomen; and of course the feeling of a bowl-ing ball sitting right atop her bladder at all times. Her breasts were tender and sensitive, and sometimes at night when she dreamt of the baby, always covered in brown hair, her breasts would leak and she would wake to see thin palebluewhite liquid on the tips of her nipples, staining the sheets.

Otherwise, her pregnancy was unremarkable. Perfectly healthy, the doctor kept saying, but for some reason the woman couldn't be-lieve her. The way the baby moved, it was like it was running away from something, twisting and turning, feet paddling so fast. Her hus-band attempted to calm her with logical explanations, but mostly he was at work, the same grocery store where the woman worked, the same grocery store where they met four years ago and fell in love in among the coconuts and pineapples, a tropical refuge amid the lake effect snow. He'd been staying later at work these days, having been promoted to assistant manager when management learned of his impending fatherhood. The woman, on the other hand, had been transferred from the produce department to the childcare room the store provided for customers, where she watched people's kids while they shopped, a glimpse into the future of her life, full of snot and tantrums and sometimes the bright spot of a sweet crayon drawing.

As her due date approached, the woman took her leave from the store. And then her due date came, and nothing happened. A week passed. The doctor said they would have to induce, but the woman wanted to wait for the baby to come on its own. Really, she was scared, biding time. She didn't feel ready. She wanted to talk to her mother, but of course she couldn't. Her mother was buried a few towns over, where the woman's grandparents had lived until they, too, passed away. Sometimes the woman tried to talk to her mother at night, to pray to her, but it always felt contrived, like she couldn't get past the fact that she was just talking to herself. Her father wasn't around, either; the week after the woman had graduated high school, her father and stepmother had moved to Florida and that's where they'd lived for nearly five years now, never visiting, only sending sunny photos to her in the deep freeze of a Midwestern winter. When he found out she was pregnant, her father began calling once a month, asking how she was doing. Fine, she always said, even if a lightning bolt of sciatica pain was shooting up her thigh. The calls were short. Let me know when the little guy is here, her father always said at the end. He assumed it would be a boy, even though they didn't know yet. They were waiting to find out; they wanted to be surprised.

Her husband hated when she put it that way, "surprised." There aren't that many options, he always said. It's not going to be that much of a surprise.

❧

The child was born covered with a light coating of brown fur. Lanugo, the doctor called it. It wasn't that unusual, she said, though more common in premature births. The woman stroked it when the child was brought to her, after she was sewn up and brought to the recovery room. The child also had a sweaty swirl of brown hair on her head, and saucer-large eyes, staring up at her. The woman stared back, willing herself to feel something for this child: love, connection, the instantaneous bond everyone said she'd feel. But all she felt was tired. How many hours, how many days had passed since she'd been brought to this hospital? She no longer knew what time of day or night it was. She held the baby to her breast, moved her nipple to the child's mouth.

The child sucked and sucked, but nothing happened. Over the next few days, doctors and nurses and midwives and lactation consultants came in and out of the woman's hospital room, a revolving door that never allowed her to sleep. The child was trying, but the woman just wasn't producing milk. A frustrated nurse plugged the baby's mouth with a bottle of formula, and the child gulped it down hungrily. Meanwhile the woman held a pump at her tits, feeling like a milked cow, the machine whirring, the suction pulling, pulling, pulling, till her nipples were numb, and at the end the vial contained one small drop of breastmilk, a tiny yellowed pearl.

She fed it to her daughter using a syringe, and when they left the hospital the next day they took home a bag of formula samples. The first two weeks she continued trying to breastfeed, lying on the couch day and night with the child strapped to her chest. Every time she tried to feed the child she became almost angry, not with the child exactly, more with herself, her body. Why couldn't it work correctly? She looked at the child and saw a stranger. In the rare times she was able to fall into a brief and dreamless sleep, she awoke terrified, disoriented when she saw the baby: who was this creature?

Eventually she gave up because the child began refusing her breast. Nipple confusion, the doctor called it. The baby wanted the bottle, so the baby got the bottle. The woman fed the baby like this, and at times in the warm afternoon, with the sunlight slanting through the windows and the apartment quiet, she even felt something close to contentment. As a month passed, then two, the world gradually came into clearer focus, like adjusting the knob on a telescope, her daughter the star she was gazing at.

How she was changing! Every day, something new. Her cheeks filling out, her first smile, her first laugh, the way she crossed her ankles when she was drinking a bottle, her body stretching the three-month-old clothes, her first time rolling over, sitting up. And then the more unusual things: when the lanugo left, the spots appeared, little white freckles on her tan skin. And her eyes, those huge eyes that started out as blue, slowly transforming every day to grey, to green, and finally, at six months, settling into a deep brown, her long dark eyelashes framing her eyes so that any time she brought the baby to the supermarket, a grandmother would inevitably cry, What beautiful eyes she has!

She was reaching milestones well ahead of what was expected, the doctor said. The woman's husband beamed with pride, but the woman couldn't help but feel a little worried. She'd begun biting her nails, and the tips of her fingers were often bloody when she smeared diaper cream on her daughter, who suffered from diaper rash and constipation. Around six months, the baby stopped having regular bowel movements and began producing hard little turds, like grape nuts, and she would have to push and push, red-faced, to get them out. In these moments more than any other, the woman felt a crushing love for her daughter. This tiny human she had brought into the world, suffering, and there was nothing she could do.

When the baby was almost a year, the woman went back to work in the produce department. They allowed her to keep her daughter in the childcare room during her shifts, watched over by the teenage clerks. It was the best solution, she and her husband decided. Still, the first time she had to leave her daughter, she cried. The baby clung to her. How excruciating it was, to peel her daughter's arms off her shoulders and place her rigid, screaming body into the arms of another person. But each time, the drop-offs became less fraught, until eventually her now-walking, now-running toddler was jumping out of her mom's arms and into the middle of the colorful carpet, doing somersaults, playing with dinosaurs, grabbing thick crayons and scribbling on pieces of paper, not looking at the woman once, even as the woman called, Goodbye! Love you! See you later!

⚞

It is commonly understood that motherhood warps time. How slow those first few weeks and months, but then sometime after a year, time starts shooting ahead at lightning speed, and the child who was once as small as a piece of fruit is suddenly eating a peach, and the child who was unable to stand up is now galloping into a field and will not come inside no matter how many times the woman calls.

Some of her daughter's changes gave the woman pause. The white spots on the girl's back faded, thankfully, when she was two years old, but the lanugo returned. Concerned, she brought the child to the doctor. They would take blood work, look into nutritional deficiencies. Probably nothing to worry about. But the doctor's eyes mirrored the woman's concern when they looked at the little girl's legs, so long and incredibly thin.

The woman's husband agreed with the doctor; their daughter was under-nourished. The problem was the vegetarian diet. He tried to get the girl to eat meat, held forkfuls of chicken or hamburger or steak in front of her mouth, but the girl refused. She ate other things, though, things she shouldn't have; she especially liked grass and flowers and leaves and pretty much any vegetation. The spring before she turned three was an especially hungry one for her; the woman would take her out to parks and have to avoid the strange looks of other moms as her daughter grabbed weeds from under the slide and tried to shove them into her mouth.

Even more than most kids, the girl wanted to be outside: she wanted to play there, eat there, sleep there. One night, she climbed out of her crib and somehow made her way outside, and it wasn't until morning, when the woman went to get her up for the day and found the crib empty and ran screaming around the house, that she finally saw her daughter through the window, curled up on the grass outside. She ran to her, shook her. What are you doing? And of course, the child cried, as all children do when fear makes their mothers into wild things. The woman embraced her daughter and told her to never do it again.

The girl was growing taller every day, her arms now almost matching her legs in how long, thin, and sinewy they were. Sometimes the girl would run around the house on all fours. The woman forced a laughed and called her silly, but a seed of worry was furiously blooming inside her. One night, the woman couldn't sleep, so she got up and wandered over to the window to look out at the moon. In the back yard, she saw a family of deer, three of them, milling around, nibbling delicately at the grass. Beside them was a smaller animal, which the woman realized with sudden horror was not an animal at all but her daughter, standing on all fours, eating grass beside them.

The woman ran outside, barefoot, the dew cool on her feet. When she approached the girl, though, she hesitated, suddenly feeling like an interloper, an unwelcomed guest interrupting a family meal. She grabbed her daughter, and the deer scattered, their white tails flashing in the night like gleaming moths.

⁂

The woman and her husband watched the girl more closely over the next few weeks, leading up to her third birthday. The woman furiously Googled her daughter's symptoms, but very little came up. Pica. Various skin conditions. Autism spectrum disorders. And strangely, postpartum depression and anxiety, as if Google were diagnosing her instead.

It wasn't all worry, though; sometimes, it was wonder. One dusk, they were sitting on the porch of the small house they had scraped to buy the previous year, mother, father, daughter, enjoying the view of the field across the street. A family of deer—the same ones the woman had seen the other night—wandered into the field and pranced, playful, chasing one another on skinny legs in the dying light. One of the deer stood on its hind legs to eat leaves from an oak tree. Another ran up and jumped, trying to grab a leaf and failing, falling over. Their daughter laughed at this, a true, full, irrepressible waterfall of a belly laugh. Then she got up and, before the woman could grab her, crossed the street and joined the deer in their strange dance in the meadow.

The woman ran to the edge of the road, but her husband told her to wait. Watch. Let the daughter do this one thing. And so they watched their tiny human daughter—the one they'd nurtured from infancy, the one they'd seen transform from infant into this strange creature, the one they'd bathed and changed and learned to love, because love wasn't something given fully formed from the beginning but something that grew over time like any ordinary houseplant— they watched this child whose hands and feet once formed in her womb, they watched those hands and feet touch the earth and blend into this other, wilder family.

❧

The girl's third birthday was a small celebration, the in-laws the only ones celebrating with them, giving concerned looks when the child refused a hamburger, reprimanding her sharply when she bent down to eat a chrysanthemum. Before they left, they urged the woman to take the girl to a doctor and the woman agreed, but her agreement was hollow. This seemed to be something beyond science, she thought, something more to do with the soul—but she did not say that, not to her in-laws or even to her husband.

They put their daughter to bed together that night, both of their arms around her as they sang their goodnight song. The woman couldn't shake the feeling that this would be the last time they would sing it. Maybe her husband knew, too, and that's why she felt his arms wrap a little tighter around the child, why they both held on a little longer.

They left the door open a crack, as they always did, and the nightlight on. The woman considered staying up all night, but she was tired, and ultimately she fell asleep. She was awoken by her husband telling her to come quick.

The back door was open. The daughter had run outside, naked, and was standing among the deer, feeding on grass in the backyard. The girl was now almost fully transformed, almost impossible to distinguish as human but for her fingers and toes that still numbered ten, like on the day she was born. The mother knew that eventually these appendages, too, would transform into hooves. The mother knew the daughter no longer belonged to them, if she ever did, and there was no going back. She knew the only thing she could do, the right thing to do, if she loved her daughter, was to let her go into the woods, into the darkness, to give her back to nature and let her live out her life there, eating and sleeping and mating and leaping, and if one day the girl returned to the field or the yard or the lip of the woods, the woman would be watching, and welcome her in.

JUBILEE YEAR

AFTER A WEEK OF traveling through the woods, Mathilde and her mother have finally gotten within view of the abbey. It is a monstrous thing, weather-worn stone, dark and foreboding, protruding from a hillside somewhere between Cologne and Ghent like an unwelcomed growth. Mathilde follows her mother up the hill toward the building with a mixture of relief and trepidation. She knows this is the last time she will see her.

She watches her mother's back, this sturdy, solid woman, this woman who has borne seven children, four of them dying at birth, the remaining two, aside from Mathilde, dead now of the disease that also killed their father and that plagued their entire village over the last year. She wants to study her mother's shape, burn it into her memory. She has heard that in the next world there are no fathers or mothers, husbands or wives. She has heard that people turn into light-forms, shadows. She wants to be able to find her mother when she sees her again, so she watches her back sway all the way up the hill, her brown-gray hair blowing in the breeze, her chapped hands gripping tightly to a basket of provisions that is to last her the whole way home.

There is no lengthy goodbye. The Abbess, a gaunt woman with a face like parchment, watches silently as Mathilde's mother bends her gray face close and kisses Mathilde's forehead. She asks Mathilde to pray for her. *I will try*, Mathilde wants to say, but instead she says, "I will." And then her mother turns the mule around and retreats into the forest.

❧

After informing Mathilde of the daily schedule of prayer—Matins at two a.m.; Lauds at dawn; Prime, Terce, and Sext between six a.m. and three p.m.; Vespers in the evening; and Compline before sleep—the Abbess instructs four sisters to show Mathilde to the dormitory so she can change into a tunic and veil. It will be some time before Mathilde takes her vows, the Abbess says, but in the interim she is to act as if she is already part of their order.

The sisters are, at first glance, identical: pinched faces under brownish-gray veils. Upon closer inspection, though, Mathilde begins to see differences. There are two sisters whose faces show them to be much older than Mathilde. The third sister is small and chubby and quite young, her voice high as a child's. The fourth sister, Else, is about the same age as Mathilde, an age that in other circumstances would be considered marriageable. Else gives Mathilde a small, secret smile, and Mathilde smiles back. It feels strange on her face, so long has it been since she has done it.

In the dormitory, the sisters place upon Mathilde's straw mattress a tunic and veil matching their own and then, without speaking, leave the room. Mathilde pulls the tunic on quickly and tries to cover her hair with the veil. Her hair—nut-brown, braided in one thick rope hanging down her back, bearing the memory of her brother who tugged it and her mother who combed it—is too long to fit completely under the veil, the bottom of it waving behind her like a tail when she finally follows the sisters to the refectory for dinner.

Mathilde sits beside Else on the long wooden bench. As the sisters pass bowls around the table, Mathilde follows Else's motions by spooning herself one ladle of stew and tearing off a small hunk of bread. Spooning the broth into her mouth, she is struck with the memory of her mother's stew. It was thick, full of meat they would pull out with flesh hooks and eat on the side, while the broth would thicken with grains and vegetables. On cold days it would warm her whole body, and her mother never put a limit on how much Mathilde could have, even if it meant she herself would go hungry that night.

Dinner is passed in silence. About halfway through, Mathilde realizes that the women are communicating through sign language. Across the table, the young chubby sister makes a circle with her thumb and forefinger. The girl's skin is pink, and she has white, almost invisible eyebrows and eyelashes. Compared to the gaunt, gray faces of the villagers Mathilde left behind, this girl resembles a well-fed pig. Mathilde does not know what the girl is signing until Else reaches over, grabs the bread basket, and passes it across the table.

Mathilde finishes before the other sisters, so she puts down her spoon and sits silently as they finish. Outside, it grows dark. The windows are open, letting in cool night air. Mathilde watches the moon slowly rise above the fields, and she thinks of home, the same moon rising above her family's hut. Her family, mostly gone now. Is this to be her new one?

There is a clatter across the table. A bowl flies past Mathilde's head, breaking on the wall. The young piggish girl had thrown it. Now she begins shrieking, hissing, climbing on the table. She points at Mathilde, calling her a witch. Mathilde recoils. The Abbess and the rest of the sisters continue to eat while a large-boned, middle-aged sister named Grede rises slowly from her seat and walks over to where the girl is thrashing on the table. Grede looks at Mathilde sharply, clearly angry with her for something, and then she pets the girl's head. This calms the girl, who snuggles into Grede's arms, rubbing against her, purring. And then, with a firm grip around the girl's torso, Grede leads her out of the room. The sisters clean up the mess calmly, saying nothing. Else picks up Mathilde's spoon and replaces it on the table face down. After they leave the room, she explains to Mathilde that the sisters believe if a spoon is left face up, the devil can enter through it. That's why the girl—Agnes—had an outburst.

The bells ring for Vespers. As the sisters walk through the glass-walled cloister, Mathilde watches two shapes moving in the night: Grede and Agnes. Grede opens the gate to the pig pen and Agnes enters, crouches on all fours, and mills among the animals. She will stay there until her spell is over.

This, Mathilde soon learns, is just part of their routine.

❧

Witch. The word is all too familiar. Mathilde was born with a veil over her eyes, her face cocooned within a caul. This rare occurrence, her mother told her, would gift her with second sight. And she was right: Mathilde could see things, sense things before they happened. Not always, and not with perfect accuracy, but she knew, for instance, when the disease visited their village that it would kill many. She could smell death in her dreams. A hilltop turned into a heap of bodies for a moment, and then back into a hilltop. She tried to warn them, the villagers, but they turned on her, accusing her of witchcraft, proclaiming that only God knew their future, and God would protect them if they were pious.

He didn't.

Mathilde watched as her neighbors, friends, brother, sister, and father all perished, and there was nothing she could do. She prayed, but He did not do anything either. Still, the accusations of witchcraft continued, even as Mathilde helped tend to the sick, prepare the bodies for burial, dig the graves. This accusation is what prompted her and her mother to leave after they had buried the last of their dead. Although there was another abbey closer to their village, her mother chose this particular abbey because, she said, she wanted Mathilde to be as far away from the pestilence as possible. By the grim smirk on her face, Mathilde knew her mother was referring not to the disease but to the people of their village. And she knew, too, that this would be the last joke her mother would ever tell her.

꙳

The days have a rhythm like the plainchants they sing during Mass. Every movement is in a single key; there are moments of rest and silence, and moments of vigorous chanting; there are hard syllables and soft syllables and round vowels that open up space in their throats and echo off the high ceilings like the voice of God calling back to them.

With the first light of dawn, Mathilde and the sisters walk to the church for Lauds. After Lauds, the priest arrives from a neighboring village to hold Mass, his voice muffled behind the wooden screen. To receive communion, the sisters approach the screen and the priest's hand emerges through a small door to drop the wafer onto their tongues.

After Mass, the Abbess leads the sisters to the chapter house where she reads a chapter of rule. It is Grede who often brings violations of rule to the Abbess's attention. One morning, Grede complains that Mathilde is not keeping her hair covered. The Abbess notes in response that Mathilde is still a novice; when she takes her vows, her head will be shorn like the rest of them. It is the first time Mathilde understands the physical reality of her transformation. The long brown hair she inherited from her mother will be gone, just like her mother is gone.

When the meeting ends, the work day begins. Mathilde follows Grede and Agnes out to the animal pens, and they spend their days shearing sheep, milking cows, collecting hens' eggs. As they work, Grede looks at Mathilde with suspicion and speaks to her only when issuing instructions. Her disposition with Agnes is softer. When Agnes spills a pail of milk, Grede does not chastise her. When Agnes stands in the middle of the pen among the sheep, staring off into the distance, Grede shakes her gently, like waking a child from sleep.

In the afternoons, Mathilde sometimes walks the cloister alongside Else. Mostly, Else tells Mathilde stories of her childhood. She had been born into a family with too many daughters, and it was cheaper to become a bride of Christ than the bride of a merchant. Besides, she tells Mathilde, the thought of marrying a man was terrifying. Her hand lightly brushes Mathilde's as they walk.

Sometimes after supper, when they retire to the dormitory, Else combs out Mathilde's hair, stroking it with such tenderness Mathilde feels like crying. Sometimes in the dark, she relaxes back into Else's arms, and a feeling comes over her that is so new, but so natural, she doesn't know what to do with it. Sometimes Else stays in her bed and they sleep curled together like spoons.

Else always sneaks out of Mathilde's bed before all the sisters wake at two a.m. Then Grede, holding a candle, leads the line of them down the night stair to the church, where the Abbess meets them for Matins. After Matins, they head back to the dormitory to rest a couple hours before dawn, but Mathilde can never fall back asleep; she thinks of her father, dead now for months, and of her mother, who has most likely fallen victim to the disease as well. Praying feels hollow, like shouting into an empty cave. She listens for God's voice but hears only the breathing of the sisters.

Once in a while, she hears someone dream-talking. It reminds Mathilde of how her sister would sometimes laugh in her sleep. Even after the disease came and their brother died and she got sick as well, even then her sister sometimes laughed at visions only she would ever know.

❧

One night when the bell rings for Matins, one of the sisters does not rise. It is Katherine, an old woman who had a white thin-skinned face with piercing blue eyes and whose gnarled hands were constantly clasped in prayer. The sisters retrieve the Abbess, who confirms what they already knew: Katherine is dead.

The Abbess tells Mathilde she is to take her vows the next morning. In order to be classified as an Abbey, she says, they need at least twelve ordained sisters aside from the Abbess, and Katherine's death makes them one short. If Mathilde does not take her vows before Katherine's funeral, the priest would use it as an opportunity to reclassify their order and provide them with less assistance. Mathilde does not feel ready, but she cannot say no.

In the morning the church is dimly lit by three candles placed around the altar. Else, standing beside Mathilde, squeezes her hand. They chant their opening prayers, and then Mathilde kneels in front of the altar and removes her veil. She sees something shining in the Abbess' hand: a pair of shears. When the first cut is made, severing the long braid, Mathilde feels unmoored. The braid lies besides her on the floor like a dead snake.

Mathilde repeats the muffled incantations of the priest, vowing chastity, poverty, obedience, the words exiting her mouth automatically, without conviction. I love Christ into whose bed I have entered, she repeats. The tiny wooden door in the screen squeaks open, and the priest's hand emerges, barely visible in the dark save for the small gold band he holds. Mathilde holds out her hand and the priest fumbles to find her fourth finger until he finally slides it on.

The priest then instructs her to lie before the altar face down as a symbol that she is dying to her old life. Mathilde spreads her body on the stone floor, nose pressed into the dirt. She has often wondered, over the past year, when and how death would come to her. When she did not die after her brother, with whom she had played, or her sister, with whom she had shared a bed, or her father, for whom she had cared in his illness, she wondered what it would take to kill her. She tries to think of the entirety of her life, but all that comes is one image from her childhood: sitting upon her father's knee, the way he taught her the alphabet by carving letters into apples, and how they would eat them afterward, sweet and crisp. Is this what people think of before they die, apples? But no, she is thinking now of her mother. Could she still be alive?

Mathilde rises. The priest, behind the screen, says a blessing and she can see his hands forming the sign of the cross. She repeats the motion, and with that, her baptism into this new family is complete.

꙼

The next morning, the Abbess tasks Mathilde with preparing Katherine's body for the funeral. Katherine's body is kept in a stone room, laid out on a wooden board, still clothed in the tunic she had been wearing when she died. When Mathilde pulls the tunic up over the sister's torso, the smell of death is so pungent it dizzies her. Her vision grows fuzzy.

In the center of this fuzzy vision, Katherine's body transforms, and suddenly it is the Abbess who is laid out before her. Dotting the length of the Abbess's torso are constellations of sores, the same sores that dotted Mathilde's brother's body, and her sister's, and her father's, and the body of every neighbor who died of the disease. Mathilde grabs onto the table to keep from falling. She looks away but the afterimage of the Abbess's body remains. When she finally looks back at the table, it is Katherine's body again, spotless. But Mathilde knows, now, that the disease is coming for them. Perhaps it is she who brought it?

This thought eats at Mathilde all day, until right before Vespers, when Katherine's funeral is to be held. Mathilde watches through the windows of the cloister as the priest rides up in the dying pink light, and it occurs to her that perhaps it is not she who has brought the illness to the abbey; it might be the priest. He might be bringing it right now.

In the silence of the cloister, Mathilde sits by each of her sisters and pleads with them not to take the Eucharist, or if they must, take it by hand rather than by tongue. They look at her, as she knew they would, outraged. Else asks why, and Mathilde wants to tell her but cannot; to do so would be to admit she knows something no one can know. Mathilde looks at Else, hoping somehow her eyes will convey all that her voice cannot, and then the bells ring out for the funeral Mass.

❧

The following Sunday, the priest never arrives. The sisters congregate in the church, but behind the screen is only silence. The next day, and the next, it is the same. Then, one morning, the Abbess does not show up for Matins or for Lauds or for Prime. The sisters search the cloister and the fields, but she is nowhere. The Abbess sleeps in a small room attached to the chapter house, where the sisters finally congregate. None of them have ever been inside the Abbess's bedroom. A quiet argument breaks out between those who want to enter the Abbess's room and those who think it unseemly. Finally, without speaking, Mathilde gets up, passes the other sisters, and opens the Abbess's door.

Mathilde is hit immediately with the smell of rot. Despite the heat, the Abbess is bundled under layers of wool. Her breath draws in and out in short, raspy waves. Her eyes open as slits amid her swollen face, which is dotted with boils. Pus drains into the corner of an eye. She blinks rapidly. When she speaks, her eyes are unfocused, trained on the ceiling. She asks Mathilde if the priest has arrived. Mathilde replies that he has not.

The Abbess closes her eyes. "Last Rites," she says.

"I can ask Grede, but—"

The Abbess shakes her head and grabs Mathilde's wrist with surprising strength. "No," she says. "You."

Mathilde wants to refuse, but how can she? She thinks of her father, dying, pleading for Last Rites, no priests left in their village. Mathilde and her mother prayed over him, hoping for some miracle, but none came. It was then that she began to wonder about God's power, or powerlessness, in their world. And if God didn't have the power to anoint the sick, then who did? The priests were all dead, proving after all that they were only human. Which meant Mathilde, human too, could become a vehicle of God's power, of His mercy.

Mathilde rushes out of the room, around the throng of kneeling sisters, through the cloister, and into the church. In the tabernacle, Mathilde finds a chalice with communion wafers, leftover wine, and a vial of consecrated oils for anointment. When she gets back to the chapter house, the sisters are arguing. Grede blocks the doorway to the Abbess' room.

"She is dying," Mathilde pleads.

"The priest will come."

"He is dead, too."

Grede pounds the wall next to the door and the room falls silent. "Have you cursed us?" she cries. "Before you came, no one died!"

The sisters murmur. Else speaks in Mathilde's defense. Agnes crouches down and crawls along the floor until she scrapes her knee and lets out a painful howl. Grede runs to her side, and Mathilde takes this opportunity to open the door to the Abbess's room. She rushes to the woman's bedside, but it is too late.

❧

Grede organizes the vote for a new Abbess. The sisters form a line, each of them whispering their vote into Grede's ear. On Mathilde's turn, she whispers the name of the oldest nun in the order. It is strange to lean so close to the sister who loathes her. When the scent of Grede's body reaches Mathilde, she pulls back. Rotting flesh. She knows it may not indicate disease; it could be an open wound from a belt of thorns or a hair shirt, or any of the other accoutrements of suffering these sisters inflict upon themselves. Still, Mathilde worries.

Immediately after votes are tallied, Grede announces that she has been named the new Abbess. She tells the sisters that despite the death of the old Abbess, they must continue on. They must do their work, say their prayers, or else the fabric of their life will unravel. It is the one thing Grede says that Mathilde can agree with.

❧

The following days proceed as usual, except that in the place of daily Mass the sisters spend extra time working the fields. Even those who normally do indoor work are outside, the growing chill making their breath more visible week by week. Then, as they near the harvest, disease strikes again: first an older sister, who dies after three days of illness; then a younger sister passes away soon after. Both bear the boils and blisters, and both scream in pain near the end, all the silent suffering of their lifetimes given voice in their last moments.

Grede seems thin, tired, worn. Her eyes grow large, her cheekbones sharp. And then, one day, as Grede stands before them at the meeting, she coughs up blood. The sisters draw back, but Grede wipes up the sputum with the bottom of her tunic, dabs at her mouth with her veil, and continues reading the chapter of rule as if nothing has happened.

The next morning, when Grede does not show up for Lauds or Prime, Agnes runs in a frenzy to find her. Standing outside the door to Grede's room is another sister, who blocks Agnes from going in. Agnes tries to push past, banging on the door, scratching the sister's face, screaming about the Devil. Else tries to hold her back, to calm her, but Agnes shoves her off. Mathilde approaches Agnes cautiously, explaining that Grede is ill, and that everyone is trying to protect Agnes by not letting her enter the room. But Agnes will not listen. Even as she calms down, she insists that Grede is not ill but possessed, that demons have entered the abbey and are taking over Grede's soul.

Her fear is infectious. One of the younger sisters, as well as the sister guarding the door, begin to murmur that perhaps Agnes is right, the illness is the doing of Satan. The sister guarding the door opens it and lets Agnes enter. The other sisters rush in behind her while Mathilde hovers in the doorway.

Upon seeing Grede, Agnes calms down. Grede, having heard Agnes's outburst, explains in a weak voice that her body is sick, but her soul is pure. She is ready for Last Rites.

She looks at Mathilde.

Mathilde stands above the bed with the chalices and holy oils. She begins by taking Grede's confession. Grede hesitates a long time before saying anything.

"Agnes," she says. "Is my…" She doesn't finish.

"I know," Mathilde says, and when Grede looks at her questioningly: "You treat her with the tenderness of a mother." Mathilde smiles, thinking of her own.

Grede's breathing becomes more shallow. Mathilde hurries to administer the Eucharist. Grede opens her eyes and looks into Mathilde's face, for the first time with something resembling kindness.

"Look after her," she says.

⊰⊱

The air grows colder, the sky sunless. The remaining sisters work together to prepare for harvest, but as the weeks wear on, two more of them die, Lyse and Delphine, within hours of each other. They are down to seven sisters. There is no vote for a new Abbess. The sisters seem aimless. Else tries to give them purpose, direction, and asks for Mathilde's help. Despite her doubts and anger and questions unanswered by God, Mathilde agrees. They begin to hold meetings, praying, discussing how to keep up with the farm work when there are so few sisters left.

On the first day of harvest, the clouds threaten a storm, but the sisters spend most of the day in the fields nonetheless, picking and threshing and gathering. The experience is a small reprieve from death. They run through the rows. They hide from one another like children. By the end of the night, the sisters are fatigued and red-faced. They sleep soundly.

They wake before Lauds to a crack of thunder. They lie in bed as the rain pours and the shutters shake and the intermittent rumble of thunder makes them jump. Agnes climbs into bed with Mathilde, and Mathilde tries to comfort her, singing her a lullaby that she remembers her mother singing. *Sleep, little sheep, sleep. The Lord fends off the murdering wolf. Sleep, little sheep, sleep.*

But Agnes does not sleep, and it is clear the other sisters are not sleeping either. Else climbs into bed with Mathilde and Agnes. She begins to say something, but her voice is drowned out by the loudest crack of thunder, and then the darkness is broken with a flash of light. One bolt of lightning, and then another, hits a tree not far from the abbey, and the tree falls into the far end of the cloister, shattering windows. The sisters scream. Hail pellets the roof. The sisters begin to murmur excitedly. Lightning, hail—these are all *signs*. The work of demons.

"Demons?" Agnes repeats. Mathilde tries to quiet her but she repeats the word until she falls asleep, and when she wakes, the word is still on her tongue.

The storm has quieted, so the sisters go to check on the damage in the cloister. It is not bad, but through the shattered glass walls they see something worse: lightning has scorched their fields. Mathilde and Else run outside and find the unharvested crops ruined. Agnes and the other sisters conclude it is the work of demons. Demons are hiding everywhere in the abbey, they say, ready to prey upon them.

Another death. A quiet sister, Hette, leaves her bed at night to die in the barn with the animals. There are now six sisters. All besides Mathilde and Else look at this number as a sign. The devil's number. At first, this obsession leads to more pious behavior. They chant more furiously at each office, they spend their free time praying, they take vows of silence. Some of them wear belts of thorns and flagellate themselves. The weeks go by in this fashion, the sisters mostly keeping to themselves, eating very little, trying to plan for the winter

ahead. They have a small amount of crops from the first day of harvest, plus animals for meat and milk.

But one morning when Mathilde and Else go to milk the cows,
they are greeted by a sight that is, at first, hard to make sense of. It
looks like animals writhing around on the ground, but it is really Agnes, Dorothea, Anna, and Liphilt, crawling over the hay on all fours,
howling, naked, wild-haired. Dorothea is in the horse stall, and when
she emerges her mouth is smeared with feces. This sight, though,
is nothing compared to what Mathilde sees next. The animals—all
of them, save for one horse—have been killed, slaughtered by these
four sisters, and left to rot. Their corpses are strewn about the barn,
bloody intestines pulled out, partially eaten.

Mathilde rushes forward and grabs Dorothea, trying to shake
her into her senses. The old woman resists, but Mathilde pulls her
out of the barn and drags her back to the cloister and finally into
the church, where she lays the woman on the stone floor and leaves
her there, running back to get the others. With Else's help, Mathilde
drags all the screaming sisters into the church. The four sisters lay on
the floor, naked, finally falling silent.

The next month is a practice in self-sacrifice. The sisters allow
themselves only one small meal a day. With their hunger, their fears
of the devil increase. They begin to see him everywhere. Most of the
sisters' time now is spent sitting in the drafty cloister, looking out the
cracked windows at the first snow. In the whiteness they see demons
tempting them to like steal food or slaughter their last remaining
horse for meat, and to ward off the demons they flagellate themselves.

As Mathilde lies in her bed at night listening to the sisters'
breathing, she is more lonely than she has been in a long time. Else
has stopped coming into her bed. Mathilde wonders if this loneliness
is a sin, a recognition that God is not with her. But she struggles to
conjure Him out of emptiness. She realizes she has felt His presence

most through the presence of those she loves: the touch of Else's body pressing against her own, the memory of her mother's scent, her father's chapped hand touching her cheek.

Then, one cold night, Else crawls back in bed with her. Mathilde, feeling small and childlike, asks Else why she has been distancing herself.

Else hesitates, and then says she is afraid the disease is beginning to take root in her. She has begun feeling feverish. And she, too, has begun seeing things.

Mathilde holds her the rest of the night, afraid to let her go. But Else is not the next to die. It is Dorothea, passing in sleep. Liphilt goes next, succumbing the following week. Immediately after she dies, Agnes and the only other remaining sister, Anna, run to Mathilde and ask if they may eat Liphilt's flesh, since they have nearly run out of food.

"Do you want to be next?" Mathilde cries, realizing it sounds like a threat.

The two sisters recoil, rolling their eyes back in their heads so that only the whites are showing, and then fall on the floor and contort their bodies.

Mathilde calls to Else for help. Else comes, out of breath. She is thin, skeletal, and Mathilde can see the sign of fever in her eyes.

"What do we do?" she asks.

"We must leave," Mathilde finally says.

❧

They hitch their last remaining horse to a cart filled with what few provisions they have left. They lay Anna, sick in mind as well as body, on the cart too, hoping the journey away from the abbey will at least calm her fears of the devil. They hope the same for Agnes, who walks beside the cart, looking in at Anna from time to time.

"Where are we going?" Agnes asks. Her face, for the first time in months, looks pink and healthy in the cold December air, her eyes clear.

Else, on horseback, looks questioningly at Mathilde.

"There is another abbey," Mathilde says. "A five-day journey. My mother and I passed it on our way here." Her voice catches on the word *mother*. So long since she has said it.

"Why did you join our order," Else asks, "if that abbey was closer to your village?"

Mathilde realizes that even though she had revealed much to Else, she had never divulged how thoroughly her community shunned her as a witch, to the point where Mathilde herself had been on the verge of believing it. But she does not want to speak of witchcraft while Agnes and Anna are within earshot.

"My mother," Mathilde finally says, "thought it best I join an order farther from our village. To be as far from the disease as possible."

A noise like a laugh comes out of Else's throat. "That did not work out in your favor, eh?"

Mathilde smiles. "I am glad to have joined your order," she says, squeezing Else's hand. They hold hands for a few minutes, Mathilde keeping pace with the horse. It feels a little like praying.

When they stop for the night, Mathilde and Agnes make a fire. Else is quiet, lying on the cart next to Anna, who has not eaten or drunk anything since the previous day. They try to entice her by placing the last of their meat close to her lips, but she will not open her mouth.

In the morning, they find Anna no longer breathing. They fold her hands over her chest and place her body under a pile of brush and leave her behind. Mathilde hopes they will reach the abbey before any other deaths befall them.

The next days wear on, bitter. It begins to snow, their footsteps leaving a trail that vanishes behind them. No matter how far they walk, the forest looks the same, tree after tree. Mathilde begins to wonder if they will ever reach the abbey. She begins to wonder if this other abbey even exists, if it were a vision she had conjured to give herself hope.

Else complains of blisters and bleeding pustules. Mathilde tries to assure her that they will soon arrive and the sisters there might have some salve to heal her, but she can see in Else's eyes that she knows the end is near.

Waking on the sixth day, Mathilde is terrified she will find that Else has died overnight. She is alive and breathing, though weak. Else pleads that they should arrive at their destination soon, not because she hopes for a cure, but because she wants to taste the Eucharist one final time. "And a strawberry," she says, smiling. "I would like to taste a strawberry one last time."

They quicken their pace, Mathilde trotting beside the horse, the three sisters silent throughout the day and into the dusk. Darkness begins to fall, but as they continue farther, the woods grow lighter. They are entering a clearing. They see a field full of brilliant, untouched snow. And beyond it, an abbey.

It is large, a cathedral and stone buildings surrounded by a gate, warm candles glowing behind stained-glass windows, snow topping its spires. They run until they reach the gate, out of breath and on the verge of collapsing. Mathilde looks at Else, to make sure she is still with them.

"We are here," Mathilde says. Else is silent, but her eyes gleam.

They stand at the gate, ring the bell, and wait. As the minutes draw on, Mathilde despairs, and her despair grows deeper as the minutes stretch to hours. What if, after all their travels, having arrived at their destination, they are left to die outside the gates?

They drift in and out of sleep. They wake sometime in the middle of the night to a messenger arriving on horseback. When the hood is pulled down, Mathilde sees the rider is a woman. She greets them and pulls out a key, opening the gate.

Another woman, this one in white, emerges from the building and greets them as if they are expected guests. The messenger rushes ahead. Mathilde and Agnes, supporting Else, hurry to the large building, where the woman in white opens the door and beckons them inside.

The room is bright with candlelight and a large fire in the hearth. Shockingly, it is full of people: dozens of sisters dressed in white tunics, wearing wreaths of flowers around their veils. And others, too: men and women and children, whole families, babies even. There is music, and a feast is laid out on a long table.

Agnes rushes forward and begins gorging herself on roast goose. Mathilde, holding Else, approaches the nearest sister.

"Sister," she says, and she does not have to say any more. The sister takes Else's body from Mathilde's arms and brings her into a nearby room, where they lay her down on a straw bed. There is a tabernacle in this bedroom, something Mathilde has never seen outside of a church before. Later, she will ask the sisters about it, and she will come to know that in this abbey, many things are different. These sisters are of the Beguine order. They marry, they preach, they have children, and they translate the Bible from Latin so all people can read it.

Else will never know the identity of these women in white. Soon after they place her in bed, Mathilde administers the Eucharist, and then places upon Else's tongue a small strawberry from the feast table. Else chews slowly, staring into Mathilde's eyes with a small smile on her face, the same small smile she gave when they first met those many months ago. She dies shortly thereafter, before dawn, warm in bed, Mathilde at her side, holding her hands. In Else's last moment, her eyes flicker with fear but also with gratitude. And although

Mathilde is filled with sorrow at the passing of the woman she loves, as she emerges from Else's room back into the ongoing feast, she feels something like light filling her body.

She approaches Agnes, who has stopped eating and is sitting comfortably on a chair among the other sisters. They are asking her where she comes from, and she is answering them, chatty as a little girl. Mathilde sits down beside her.

Agnes turns excitedly to Mathilde and exclaims, "Pope Clement just announced a jubilee to honor those who've survived the year!"

Mathilde has lost her first family, and most of her last. But the room is glowing with an amber light that reminds her of the hearth of her childhood, and the people—more people than she has seen in a long time—are clustered close together in groups of sadness and celebration, some crying, some embracing, some laughing, some dancing. In the crowd of dancing bodies, Mathilde notices one body in particular, a shape she recognizes from behind, a shape so familiar she could have found her in the dark. Mathilde does not move but watches the woman for a long time, afraid to be wrong. Mathilde watches the woman dance, swinging side to side as from joy to grief and back again, and when the music ends, when the woman finally turns around, it is her mother's face that greets her, and Mathilde rushes into the cradle of her arms.

THE MERMAID AND THE
PORNOGRAPHER

THE MERMAID IS DYING, beached on the Malibu shoreline. The pornographer spots her while picking up trash from the all-night party celebrating the release of his S&M flick, *Citizen Pain*, third in his failing series of pornographic remakes of classic movies. He drags garbage bags behind him and walks over to investigate the bright lump of flesh, which in the distance resembles a beached dolphin or seal. At first he thinks it's just the gray light of morning or the milky cataracts forming in his eyes, but up close it's unmistakable: It's a real mermaid. Gorgeous. And naked.

Her top half looks as human as the actresses in his movies, only the mermaid's tits are real, her nipples so pale they're nearly invisible. Her stomach is smooth, no bellybutton, her hair long, scalloped waves that flow down over her body and end in a calligraphic spiral, its color the deep indigo of spilled ink. But her bottom half is one long, thick, scaly tail, extending a good five feet from hips to flipper. It's green, but a kind of green the pornographer has never seen in life: glittering, not one color but many, all the shades of springtime and summer, all the shades of the sea when its color shifts under the sun.

The mermaid doesn't notice him. She's trying to drag herself back into the water. Her arms are small and thin, her tail heavy. The pornographer inches closer, and it occurs to him that this mermaid is a huge discovery, more important than any soap star turned adult film actress.

He glances around the beach. No one. He wonders if he alone was meant to find her, if this is the break he's been wishing for these past few years as his fame dwindled, his movies failed, and age added new pains to his body every day. He calls out a greeting.

The mermaid twists her body, looks at him. Her eyes are greenish gold, like the stain his fake gold watches used to leave around his wrist before he could afford real ones. She glances at his bare feet, then twists back and drags herself more desperately toward the waves, her tail leaving a line in the sand.

The pornographer tells her to wait, leans forward until he's close enough to touch her. A smell emanates from her, a mixture of dank woman and fresh mackerel, and she utters tiny cries that sound like bird chirps or fake orgasms. He waves a hand in front of her face, says hello again.

She stares at him, her face blanched, lips turning from coral to marble. He kneels in the sand.

"Do you understand English?" he says to her, real slow, like how he used to talk to his housekeeper, before he found out she was born in the U.S. and speaks better English than he does.

The mermaid cocks her head.

"That's okay." The pornographer laughs. "You're not the only one here that can't speak English."

He waits for her to laugh and is disappointed when she doesn't. He wonders if mermaids even have the ability to laugh. He considers that maybe she was offended by his joke since it wasn't politically correct. She continues staring at him eerily, not blinking, like she's accusing him of something. He stands up, takes a step away from her.

"What? What do you want me to do?"

Her slim arms buckle and her top half falls to the sand. Her eyelids flutter, then close.

The pornographer stands above the mermaid, watches as the tide skims the tip of her tail. There's no time to think, and he doesn't. He moves automatically, as if in a dream, picking up the mermaid's limp body off the beach, slinging her over his shoulder, stuffing her into a trash bag and into his backseat, and driving faster than he ever has back to his home in the hills.

When he takes the mermaid out of the bag, her face is blue. But then he dumps her into his fish tank that spans the length of the wall, and after a minute or so she begins moving again, twisting and twirling around the colorful fins of his exotic fish, her body looking both alien and utterly natural in that artificial seascape.

❧

The pornographer was four years old when he first saw a nudie magazine jutting out from under his father's mattress like a rock from the hazy-blue mountains that surrounded their small Kentucky town. His first vivid memory is a dark-haired woman with huge breasts, a full bush, and a snake wrapped around her torso. When his father found out, he spanked him, then sat him down on the torn and faded flowers of their couch and said gently, "That stuff ain't real. None of them women is real. Remember that."

Years after his father's death, after moving out of their poor town to Vegas and then to Hollywood, the pornographer finds his father's words true, partly. The actresses in his movies have fake tits. Fake noses. Fake lips. And yet they're very real, women you can drink and joke with. Lately, the pornographer has begun to think of other ways the word *real* can be interpreted. The actresses he films fuck men and women for money, some even enjoy it and have real orgasms. But always when the shoot ends, they wipe the makeup from their faces and look at him with glazed eyes as they say goodbye, then drive off to their own houses, lovers, children, and friends, their foreign lives in the Valley, far below the hills where he lives—and that distance is what makes the women he spends his days with seem less than real. Makes his own life seem less than real.

When he saw the mermaid on the beach, the question of if she was real or not didn't enter his mind. She was so visible, so tangible, so palpable. And she was dying. Certainly, impending death proves the existence of a person or thing, and this is what the pornographer reminds himself as he watches the mermaid twirl around in his tank that first night.

But he doesn't have time to dwell on these thoughts. Instead, he thinks about finding a bigger space for the mermaid to swim. The pornographer calls his pool guy, has him come over the next morning to drain the whole thing, replacing chlorinated water with salt water mimicking the Pacific Ocean.

Once it's ready, the pornographer transfers the mermaid to the pool. She struggles, almost slipping out of his arms, whipping her tail against his legs, beating his back with her frail fists. Poolside, he throws her into the water with a splash. He worries he has thrown her too hard because she doesn't move, just sinks. But then he sees her slowly scale the bottom of the pool, face down, smelling it. She swims faster and faster until she's gliding swiftly through the water, flipper wagging like a happy dog's tail. The pornographer is happy, too.

He sleeps that night in a rusty beach chair beside the pool. In the middle of the night he wakes to the sound of howling in the distance. He's chilly, has a crick in his neck. He glances over at the pool to make sure the mermaid is still there, and fear jolts him when he doesn't see ripples on the water's surface. But when he gets up and peers into the pool, there she is, lying on her back on the bottom, staring up at him with unblinking eyes, her hair flowing back so the protruding gills behind her ears are exposed, undulating like little murmuring mouths on the sides of her head. He waves at her. She doesn't wave back, but tendrils of her hair seem to wave, and so he sits back down in the chair and settles again into sleep. How comforting it is to have someone else with him during the night, even if she isn't quite human.

⁂

The next day, the pornographer's business partner stops by to go over figures for the sale of their most recent films. This man has been by his side since the pornographer's beginning in Vegas, when he shot his amateur movies in the back of a van, when women had full bushes and real breasts and no one used condoms. But the pornographer can't bring himself to tell his partner about the mermaid. She's a secret he wants to keep.

They sit on the pornographer's old leather sofa, cans of beer sweating in their palms, and talk about *Citizen Pain*. It just isn't selling, his partner says, just like *Tits a Wonderful Life* and *Rear Widow* both bombed. There's just no market for these movies, he says. Free sites like Pornhub were putting them out of business. He'd do better just to give up on this venture and move on to something more popular. Barely legal. Old women. BBW. Bukkake.

The pornographer laughs. "So I guess that's a no-go for *The Passion of Joan's Ars*?"

"If you want to get your career back," his partner responds, "just find a new project."

The pornographer sighs, touches the thinning hair on top of his head. "I'm out of ideas," he says. "I'm out of ideas and hair."

His partner laughs, slaps him too hard on the back, and brings his empty beer can into the kitchen. The pornographer reclines, lets the ceiling fan blow through the buttons of his satin shirt. Growing up, he never lived in a place with ceiling fans; on hot summer days his mother would simply blow air through her lips onto the back of his neck, a comforting cool, not like air conditioning, which gives his hands a bluish tint.

The pornographer hears his partner toss the can into the recycling bin, the suction of the fridge, the snap of him opening another beer. Then the clatter of the can hitting the linoleum and beer foaming out, and his partner exclaiming, "What the hell?"

The pornographer runs into the kitchen. Too late. His partner has spotted the mermaid through the window, and he's already gone outside to get a better look. The pornographer follows. As they approach, the mermaid leaves her spot poolside and dives back underwater. The pornographer and his partner are silent for a long time, watching the mermaid swim back and forth.

"I found her on the beach in Malibu," the pornographer says. "A few days ago."

His partner looks up at him. "Is it…real?"

"Can't you tell?"

"I don't know." His partner pauses. "It could be an actress with a snorkel."

"Does it look like she's using a snorkel?"

"They're doing crazy things with plastic surgery these days. You know that."

"She's real," the pornographer repeats.

"You know the story of the Fiji Mermaid?"

The pornographer shakes his head.

"Well, some circus owner sewed a monkey head and torso onto the tail of a big fish, and advertised it as a real mermaid. Monkey lived for a couple days like that, then died."

"Come closer," the pornographer says, pulling his partner to the edge of the pool. "No stitches, see? This isn't some kind of circus-sideshow shit. This isn't something I made up. I just happened to find her."

The pornographer and his partner are silent again, watching the mermaid's body snake through the water, watching as she pulls herself up to rest on one of the steps and slowly combs her hair with her fingers, untangling it so that it rests in perfect waves over her breasts.

"This is it," his partner says.

"This is what?"

"*This* is what's going to bring our careers back from the dead." He laughs, punches the pornographer's arm. "I don't know if she's real or not, but she's our new star. This is the project you've been waiting for."

The pornographer looks at the mermaid, hesitates before responding. "I'm not sure about that. Logistically. I don't even know how mermaids fuck, if they *can* fuck. Besides—"

His partner cuts him off. "We'll worry about that later. There are ways around it. Oral. Tittie-fucking. You know."

Before his partner leaves, the pornographer agrees to meet again the next day to further discuss the new project. He can't say no; he's got no real reason to. But when he sees the mermaid still combing her hair, he feels like he's wronged her in some way he can't explain. He feels like a child looking at dirty magazines, guilty. He wishes the mermaid would go back underwater, stop combing her hair. He wants this secret hidden again, at least for the rest of the day.

❧

When the pornographer rummages through his fridge that night for dinner, he realizes he hasn't fed the mermaid at all since the day he found her. He looks through the kitchen window at the pool glowing in the sunset, rippling with the movement of the mermaid under its surface. He imagines she must be starving. But what do mermaids eat? He pushes aside leftover pizza, wheatgrass juice he's started drinking to stay healthy, cartons of Chinese food, then finds a wilting salad his housekeeper put together for him. He picks out the limp greens, lays them on the counter. Then he forages through his freezer, drags out some old fish sticks, thaws them in the microwave. He takes the lettuce and the fish sticks out to the pool.

The mermaid has pulled herself out of the water and sits on the edge of the pool, her face lifted to the sky, which sheds red light over the hills and tints her eyelids violet. Sexy, he thinks, and then shakes his head. The entirely wrong word. The mermaid opens her eyes, stares at him as he walks towards her, and he feels naked under her gaze. When he gets close, she dives back into the water.

He sits on the edge of the pool, dangles his feet in. The mermaid's fear of him feels like rejection, something he isn't used to feeling, something he remembers feeling in high school until he dropped out, eloped with his girlfriend, and moved to Las Vegas, where they made their first porno together. Eventually his wife rejected him, too, leaving him for some young actor, but at that time he was at the peak of his career, and he had no shortage of women. Both his career and his love life went downhill from there. Besides his housekeeper—and the mermaid—he hasn't had a woman at the house in years.

He feels something tickle his feet and looks down to see the mermaid touching his toes, pulling them apart, sniffing them, biting his pinkie toe gently as if to see if it's edible. He pulls his feet away involuntarily, giggling. He's not sure he's ever giggled in his adult life. Looking at his feet, he regrets that he hasn't recently cut his toenails. The mermaid floats around him, not touching him anymore, but as she sways in the water a tendril of her long hair brushes one of his feet, a tendril more silky and soft than anything he's felt in his life, moonlight made tangible. The mermaid swims away.

"Wait!" he calls, waving the fish sticks and lettuce above the water. The mermaid swims back toward him and grabs the fish sticks with her mouth and the lettuce with both her little fists. He notices the mermaid doesn't have fingernails—her fingers end with smooth white flaps of skin. He's fascinated.

The last time he felt this way was as a child, watching his father gut a black bear. The bear's jaws were magnificent, open, and in its splayed stomach, his father showed him things the bear had eaten from their own garbage can: corn on the cob, apple cores, even gooey pieces of the newspaper they sometimes used as placemats at the dinner table. He was amazed at the secret treasures that could be found in an animal's stomach, and for a time afterward he'd squint at the bellies of all animals and all people he met, trying to imagine what they were hiding inside their stomachs. Of course, he stopped doing that when he became a teenager and the surfaces of things—particularly women—were much more interesting. But now, again, he stares at the mermaid, nibbling fish sticks underwater, and he wonders what's inside her.

The pornographer sleeps in his bedroom and checks on the mermaid periodically throughout the night while smoking cigarettes on the balcony. Most of the time she's floating slowly, face down or face up, on the bottom of the pool. But one time, as the clouds part to reveal the fullness of the moon, the mermaid lifts herself up to the edge of the pool, and, hair dripping behind her, she throws her head back and angles her body to the moon, the way human girls angle their bodies to the sun, except her body—tail included—is more sexy than any human girl he's ever seen. Stubbing out his cigarette, he has the nagging feeling again that *sexy* is the wrong word. He's not sure she belongs in a porno.

He watches her comb her hair with her fingers. She seems more real than the human actresses he works with every day, and maybe that's why he's uneasy about putting her in one of his movies. Clouds begin to veil the moon again, and the mermaid slips back into the water soundlessly, without a splash. The pornographer goes back to bed, thinking about his father, wondering what his father would think of the mermaid, if his father would try to convince him that, like the first naked woman he saw in a magazine, the mermaid isn't real either.

⅋

When the pornographer's partner comes back the next day, he brings with him a screenwriter friend, whose reaction to the mermaid is skepticism that transforms rapidly into awe that transforms rapidly into business. The pornographer mentions to his partner that he's still not one hundred percent sure they should use the mermaid, but his partner dismisses his worries, says he's getting too conservative in his old age.

They sit down at a table poolside and storyboard the porno while the mermaid swims in circles, eating stray crumbs of fish sticks. They decide to do a very loose take on *The Little Mermaid,* and, despite his qualms, the pornographer begins to get excited about filming it because it's something new, something he's never done before.

Over the next few weeks, the pornographer meets frequently with his partner and the screenwriter to work on the details of the movie, so absorbed in his work that he sometimes forgets the mermaid is still there. One day, he returns home from a meeting to find his housekeeper standing by the pool, screaming a scream more real than anything in the movies, a dropped mug broken at her feet. The pornographer can only guess how long his housekeeper has been standing there staring at the mermaid, who's holding onto the side of the pool, head above water, staring directly back at her.

The pornographer has forgotten his housekeeper was supposed to come today; he forgot to tell her to take this week off, too, as he had the last couple weeks. As he approaches, his housekeeper jerks her head up, stops screaming. She points at the mermaid, says nothing.

The pornographer gently grabs his housekeeper's arm, pulls it down, and then turns her body away from the pool. He's surprised at how soft and warm the skin of her arm feels, and what it arouses in him: it's been so long since he's touched a woman, so long of only watching them, filming them. For a moment he's painfully attracted to her, and even more painfully aware that this woman, in her seven years of working for him, has known him more intimately than his ex-wife, the mundane kind of intimacy that comes from washing someone's underwear.

As he leads her into the dim house, he tries to think of ways to explain the presence of the mermaid. Before he can say anything, the housekeeper speaks.

"Is she real?"

Her voice is small, timid, as his own voice must have been when he was four years old and found his dad's porno and asked him what it was.

The pornographer swallows hard, considers how to answer.

"If I said yes, would you believe me?"

Her eyes are wide, greenish-brown, sea-colored. He still has his hand on her arm. She nods. "I think I would."

"Then, yes," the pornographer responds. "She's real."

There's silence save for the sound of the refrigerator humming. Finally the woman says, "Why do you have her here? Shouldn't she be in the ocean or something?"

The pornographer lets go of her arm. Her eyes are on him, accusatory.

"I found her. On the beach. In Malibu."

"So why don't you put her back in the ocean?"

"I can't now. I need her."

He searches for the right words. The housekeeper backs away from him.

"You need her for what?"

The pornographer follows her as she walks backward into the foyer.

"Nothing bad," he says, gently grabbing her wrist again as she nears the front door.

"I have to go home early today," she says, pulling her arm away and grabbing her purse from the coat rack.

The pornographer follows her out to the driveway, asks if she's coming back tomorrow.

She shakes her head no, gets into her car. He runs up to the open passenger's side window, begs her not to leave, not to quit.

"I need you here," he says.

She sighs.

"I'll increase your salary," he tells her. "I'll let you stay here with me."

The housekeeper shakes her head again. "I can't stay here with you. I've got a husband and baby at home."

The pornographer backs away. It occurs to him that after all the years of her cleaning his house, he knows nothing about this woman's life. He wonders why the loss of this particular housekeeper is hitting him so hard, why he feels the urge to hold onto her tighter than he held onto his own wife.

"I'm sorry," he says.

"Don't be sorry," she says. "Just do the right fucking thing."

She starts her car, and it sputters away. Before she exits the drive, she calls something the pornographer can't understand out the open car window. It sounds a little like *Good luck*, but more likely it was *Go fuck yourself*. He wishes she had shouted something else, like *I'll miss you*. Or *You are forgiven*.

※

The pornographer feels the loss of the housekeeper like the loss of an invisible companion. He sits poolside as the mermaid swims back and forth, and though he knows she can't hear him under all that water, he complains to her about the mess the house is in, how quiet it is without the sound of the vacuum running at all hours of the day. He calls the agency, and they send him a new housekeeper. But this one feels different, and it's only a matter of time before she catches a glimpse the mermaid, too. Already, her second day on the job, he catches her running away from the kitchen window, feather duster fluttering behind her like wings. He worries about what she might have seen, who she might tell.

But he doesn't have time to dwell on it; it's time to shoot the film. The first day, the pornographer gets up before dawn, ready to transfer the mermaid from the pool to a small tank in order to take her to a deserted stretch of beach owned by one of his former leading porn stars. But when the pornographer gets to the pool, the mermaid is gone. He squints into the cloudy water. Gone. He searches the small wooded area behind the pool. No sign of her. When he gets to his garage, he sees that the tank is also gone.

He speeds down the hills to the coastline. As he drives to the set, he's not sure what he wants to find, whether he wants the mermaid to be there or not. So when he gets to the beach and sees the mermaid in the tank, head held above water by two assistants while a makeup artist dusts powder over her face, he's simultaneously relieved and angry and sad. He slumps in his director's chair. His partner hands him a coffee, explains they had to take the mermaid earlier than expected to do hair and makeup.

"Someone could've mentioned that to me," the pornographer says.

He looks over at the mermaid getting her hair done. When the hairdresser begins to snip the ends of the mermaid's hair, the mermaid begins to shriek as if in pain, and she thrashes around in the water, but there's nowhere for her to escape to. The pornographer stalks over to the tank, asks the hairdresser what he thinks he's doing.

The hairdresser keeps cutting the writhing mermaid's hair, muttering, "Only a trim, baby, only some layers."

The pornographer grabs the hairdresser's wrist, takes the scissors from his hand, says, "Her hair was fine the way it was."

The pornographer doesn't realize how loudly he's spoken until he looks around and sees his partner, the cameramen, his lead actor, even the fluffer all stop what they're doing and stare at him. He apologizes to the hairdresser, but the hairdresser walks off the beach in a huff, calling back, "This movie'll be a flop anyway, like the rest!"

The crew is silent. The pornographer says, "Let's get started."

But no one moves from where they're standing. The pornographer wonders why no one listens to him anymore. Is it the gray hair? The new gut? The blue veins in his legs?

"We're starting now!" he shouts, and finally the cameramen get behind their cameras, the lead actor stops getting his dick prepped and takes his place, the assistants get out of the shot.

The pornographer takes the mermaid out of the tank; she's slippery in his arms. He carries her this time, for the first time, like a baby rather than a captive. And he wonders how it would feel to hold a real baby in his arms, how it would have felt to live that real life:

a wife, children, a dog, a house cradled in the mountains, far away from the polluted coast, the plastic people, the congested highways. He looks down at the firm breasts of the mermaid and thinks of his own wrinkled chest covered with white hair. His chance to live that other life has passed.

He puts the mermaid gently down on the sand, a few feet from the water. She looks drained, pained, keeps grabbing at the ends of her hair as if to stop some kind of bleeding. An assistant kneels just out of the shot with a spray bottle to keep the mermaid wet during the shoot.

The pornographer gets behind his camera, hesitates a moment before he says *Action*. The mermaid flounders around on the sand as she did when he first found her. Her movements are more desperate than sexy. But still, as she moves, her breasts bounce like real breasts do. He waits for her to stop struggling. She doesn't. As he continues shooting, moving the camera up and down the mermaid's body, the pornographer thinks only about the curve of her breast, her scaly hip, her rouged nipples pointing to the sky. The camera gives him distance, makes the mermaid seem less real, so that he doesn't see the light fading in her eyes even as the light of dawn grows brighter.

Dressed like a sailor, the lead actor staggers down the beach, and the pornographer sees the actor's eyes grow wide, a look of real awe stopping him momentarily before he resumes his swagger and grabs the mermaid. His orchestrated movements clash with the mermaid, who squirms under his grip, his mouth, his body. The mermaid's tail sparkles against the actor's dull skin, the glare of it angry in the pornographer's eyes as he watches her struggle with her slim arms to push the actor off, her chirps and squeals growing louder. The pornographer, accustomed to the sounds of mingled pleasure and pain and fear, doesn't stop filming until his partner walks up behind him and whispers, "You've got to find some way to shut her up."

The pornographer feels shaken awake. He yells *Cut* and the actor promptly gets off the mermaid. The mermaid stops struggling, lies still and silent on the beach, pale, the water from the spray bottle not enough to sustain her. The actor backs away from her, saying, "I didn't do anything, I didn't do anything wrong." The set grows silent and the crew gathers around the mermaid, whose arms are limp above her head.

Suddenly, the mermaid sits up, looks at the clouds on the horizon, opens her mouth, and sings.

The sound is like nothing the pornographer has ever heard. The mermaid's voice is fluid, mellifluous, the flowing of her hair made audible. But it also penetrates too deeply, makes the pornographer feel like his internal organs have been pierced and their fluids are filling up his body, drowning him from the inside. The mermaid sings for the duration of a long breath, lips turning blue around the edges, and then she falls back into the sand.

The pornographer pushes through the crowd, kneels beside the mermaid. Her veins are tracing hard purple rivers in her pale face. Her eyes are still open but unfocused. The tide rolls up against the pornographer's bare feet and over the mermaid's tail, which glitters as it touches the water. The pornographer puts his arm under the mermaid's head and turns around.

"We're done here," he shouts. "Everyone go home."

He expects arguments, questions, at least from his partner. But everyone remains silent, stunned speechless by the mermaid as if her dying has made her real to them for the first time.

But the mermaid is not dead. As the crew packs up and leaves, the pornographer leans his head down over the mermaid's chest. What he hears is similar to a heartbeat, but less thumping and more flowing, less like a human heart and more like the sound of an invisible waterfall heard through a rock wall. He glances over at the tank, considers bringing her back to his pool. But how can he be sure she won't die there? And having a dead mermaid in his pool seems even worse than having a dead human being. A dead mermaid is more like a dead child, something helpless, the responsibility too much for him.

The pornographer picks up the mermaid. Her body is heavier than ever, as if the man lying on top of her somehow added his weight to hers. The pornographer wades into the waves, up to his knees, then his belly, then his chest, holding the mermaid the whole time, her tail no longer stiff but draped limp over his arm, a wilted stem. He walks farther, but he's on a sand bar, and despite how long he walks the water stays at heart level. His arms begin to ache, then his legs, all his muscles tired. He's tired. Tired of walking, tired of being a man, a pornographer, a human being. Tired of two legs. How he wants to grow fins, live in a less solid world.

The pornographer walks on, carrying the mermaid in his arms. He strays farther and farther from shore, until he glances back and the houses in the hazy distance resemble the mountains of his childhood. He takes another step, another breath—and then the ocean floor drops out below him and he sinks, the weight of the mermaid bearing down on him as he's swept away by the tide.

THE PRESERVATION OF OBJECTS LOST AT SEA

It HAS BEEN NEARLY thirty years since Greta visited Scarborough Harbor, and it's completely changed. Until her little sister's death, she vacationed every childhood summer in this tiny coastal Maine town. It used to be quaint, but now shops line the sidewalks like sharks' teeth while tanned teenagers rollerblade by in neon bikinis, and arcades flash like ambulance lights down the length of the boardwalk, dappling plastic palm trees that decorate the pebbled lawns of cheap motels. Greta is relieved by this new ugliness. It means she can pretend it's a different town altogether, one that holds no memories, good or bad.

When they pull up to the cottage, wind-washed stone and purple shutters, Ray squeezes her hand before getting out of the car, his way of apologizing for suggesting they come here. Months ago, they talked casually about a summer vacation, and he suggested this town of her childhood, this town that holds her sister's ghost. He'd said: It's time, Gret. You need to make peace. And she'd agreed, though she had no idea until they pulled into town exactly what she'd agreed to. Ray reaches over, rubs her back. This, she knows, is his way of telling her to relax, to have a simple, fun week with their daughter, Juniper, who might never come on vacation with them again, who is going to college in the fall, though Greta doesn't want her to, though Greta will do anything to keep her from going away.

❧

Kaimu still wakes up gasping sometimes, afraid he's drowning in dreams, always the same one. In the beginning of the dream, he's ecstatic as he winds the winch to pull up the heavy net, thinking of everything he might do for his family once he sells whatever it is he's caught, a prize-winning cod, a school of striped bass, a shark, a bed of pearl-filled oysters. He winds and winds for what seems an eternity, forearms shaking with effort. The sky darkens as if it is going to storm, and he knows he has to get the net back on the boat before the storm hits or else he's going to have to head for the dock and he'll lose whatever he's caught. But he keeps winding and, finally, the net tumbles over the side of the boat and flops aboard.

When he peers inside, it's not oysters or shark or bass or cod: it's the body of a girl, the bloated blue body of a girl, pale veiny fish with bulging eyes and frozen-open mouth. In the distance a tsunami-sized wave forms. Kaimu knows in a moment it will wash over them, and he will be tangled with the girl in the net, he will be dead with the girl in the net.

All of that happened, except for the tsunami, nearly thirty years ago, when Kaimu had just inherited his father's fishing boat along with the burden of taking care of his mother. The girl was Hannah Hale, a name Kaimu has never forgotten, even after raising three children of his own with his wife, Mai.

"There, there," Mai says now, wiping away the sweat on his forehead with her cool, smooth palm, her sea-stone palm. "There, there. It was only a dream."

❧

Greta is fine for days, sits on the beach watching Juniper jump waves, watching Juniper's back stiffen when a couple boys approach her, watching Juniper through cheap sunglasses she bought at the general store, watching Juniper through binoculars Ray used years ago when he went hunting until Greta told him it bothered her too much to imagine him gutting deer and moose, bringing home bloody slabs of meat, how much room they took up in the freezer.

Greta is fine, even sometimes takes her eyes off Juniper to do a crossword puzzle or walk down the shoreline with Ray, never too far. Greta is fine, until she hears the bells of the ice cream man.

She forgot how those bells make her shiver. Worse than the slow winding of muted music as the truck creeps down the street, the bells are a cold noise, and the last noise, possibly, that her sister heard. Hannah was only eight years old, and Greta was twelve, when it happened. Their parents had left them alone on the beach for an hour with the instruction that Greta was to watch after her sister, and she did, for a while. But when the ice cream man rang his bells, Greta was talking to a group of teenagers around the lifeguard station and sent her sister off alone with a dollar bill. She never saw Hannah again. That is, until her body was found by a local fisherman and readied for the funeral, fat with seawater and made up so that she looked like a caricature of herself, a dark double Greta never knew and would never know. In her mind, her real sister still floated somewhere out in the sea, among seaweed and coral, or maybe she still walked the streets in search of the elusive ice cream man. Or she might not be doing any of those things, but the girl in the casket certainly wasn't her, Greta was sure of it.

She calls Juniper back to the beach blanket, and she runs up, sand sprayed on her shins, thighs muscular from soccer, but still so pale and soft, her girl. Greta tells her daughter they need to go back to the house. The tinkle of the bells makes anxiety tingle down her sides, up the backs of her legs. The expanse of sea and sky dizzy her, and she knows only that she needs the enclosed architecture of the house, a safe space. Juniper asks why they have to leave, says it's only noon, asks why can't she just hang out at the beach alone. She looks at her mother with searching eyes, eyes that reflect the whole landscape, too much of the landscape. Ray looks at Greta also, and for a moment she thinks she'll calm down, she'll let her girl run back down to the waves.

But then the bells ring again. She tells Juniper no, she can't stay here alone, tells her husband they need to leave. She folds the blanket messily, and Juniper sighs, jams her feet into flip-flops, the ones Greta loves because they hold the shadow of her daughter's toes even when she's not wearing them.

※

After years of fishing, casting and hauling nets and winding winches, Kaimu is cursed with arthritis and has retired his business to his second-oldest son, his eldest having flown south one winter to never return except for occasional holidays. Kaimu still sometimes goes out on the boat alone, just to enjoy the way the waves rock his body. It feels natural, the rhythm, more natural than land with its static quality, its hard flat lines. Sometimes he'll drop a net just to see what he'll bring up, and more often than not it's a plastic bucket, or a tampon, or pop bottles, or a clump of mussels twisted with fishing line. But once in a while he'll bring up treasures. For instance, small stones that glow like honey. And sea glass, a huge collection of which he's amassed over the years. It comes in all colors: blue, green, brown, red, orange, white, translucent, sometimes all of those swirled together. It can be thick or thin, smooth or sharp. Sometimes Kaimu reads faint inscriptions in the glass that has more recently been shaped by the waves: Seagrams, Jack Daniels, Wild Turkey, Jim Beam. Always whiskey, Kaimu imagines, because this must be the kind of place that calls for whiskey drinking.

He did his share of drinking those years ago, after finding the girl's body, and not just to block out the image of the girl, so small but so heavy with water, mouth open in perpetual plea. The other reason was because they thought he did it, at first—he was taken in for questioning a total of three times, even held in a cell overnight. Down the hall he could hear the wailing of a woman, and he wondered if it was the girl's mother. He remembers, at the time, feeling stunned how the woman down the hall sounded exactly like his own mother, how she wailed when her husband died, and he wondered at the time if all women throughout history sound exactly alike when they cry, no matter their age or where they are from or the reason they are crying.

Eventually they let Kaimu go when they found a better lead. He never did find out who the crying woman was.

⁊⁊

Juniper begs Greta to go out even though it's going to storm. It's one of their last nights of vacation. Greta watches the Weather Channel a lot back home but does so obsessively when she's at the beach. A strong storm is supposed to rip down the coast tonight. She knows how quickly these things can approach, how the rarest disasters can happen, how even Maine can get hurricanes. She lived through one, when she was a kid and her sister was just a baby. They all cuddled on the couch, so cozy, and told scary stories when the power went out. Amazing, how even in the midst of the worst storm she felt safe, then.

The Weather Channel says gale-force winds, says the possibility of rogue waves, says heavy rain and golf-ball-sized hail. Juniper argues that it probably won't be that bad, and besides, it might not hit until morning. Greta knows she's right, but there's just no telling with these things. She tells her daughter that if she just wants to get out of the house, they can go out for pizza together.

"Don't you think," Juniper responds, "that maybe I just want to get away from you for one night?" And then she slams her door.

Greta hates when Juniper does that, and she's been doing it a lot lately, when Greta chastises her for coming home after ten, for not calling, for smelling faintly like smoke or beer. The door slam is a slap in the face, effectively puts Juniper farther away from her than ever, in another world.

"She met some friends," Ray tells her, quiet-voiced Ray.

"Boys," Greta clarifies.

"You gotta let her go."

Greta grabs a blanket from the couch, lays it over her sunburned knees, puts her head in her hands. Ray shuts off the Weather Channel and opens the curtains so Greta can feel the tepid breeze, tells her to look at the sky: it's a beautiful dusk, not threatening. But there is one cloud on the horizon, Greta points out—and it's a big one.

"Just one cloud," he says, "and you're going to let it ruin your daughter's vacation? Just let her go for a few hours. She needs this, Gret. She only gets to be eighteen once."

This is the most vocal Ray has been about Juniper in years. Greta always decided the rules, and Ray went along because he knew about her past, about her sister, about how Greta spent her whole thirteenth year not leaving the house, about how her parents never blamed her for her sister's death, not really, but she felt responsible anyway.

Greta walks over to the window, leans down on the sill, inhales. Ray is behind her, running his knuckles up and down her spine, and she imagines herself a dinosaur skeleton, something slowly becoming fossilized. She stands up straight, goes and knocks softly on Juniper's door. When she tells Juniper she'll let her go out, but only for a few hours, Juniper hugs her so tight she feels her ribs cave. Her gratitude is overwhelming—almost enough to make Greta okay with her decision.

⁂

The girl Kaimu dredged from the ocean was later found to be the first victim of a serial killer—one who posed as an ice cream man to lure children, both girls and boys, to his truck, where he molested and killed them by strangling them with fishing line and throwing them in the sea. He wasn't caught until nearly two years later, when his sixth victim survived and identified him in a lineup. Kaimu read all the articles and watched all the newscasts about the case, at once relieved his name was cleared and bitter that they suspected him at all. He knew it was because he was Japanese, that even decades after the war those men were still suspicious of his kind, were taught by their fathers to be vindictive.

Kaimu rarely thinks about the ice cream man, now, though some mornings when he strolls the beach after storms, wading through washed-up shells and stones to find something special, he hears bells in the distance and feels a chill. He read in the newspaper that the men in the lineup were all dressed in the costume of an ice cream man so the boy would be better able to identify the killer. White pants, white button-down shirt, red-and-white striped hat, an image Kaimu still can't dredge from his mind. He imagined they all looked so alike he doesn't know how the boy could pick one out. But thinking about it now, Kaimu understands well how a person's face, seemingly indistinct, can be burned into one's memory through fear, as if fear is a soldering iron, a branding tool, something that preserves.

⁂

Greta doesn't sleep, can't sleep until she knows her daughter is sleeping under the same roof. She lies under sandy sheets next to Ray, whose snoring mimics the in and out of the tide, and she wonders what Juniper is doing. She remembers when Juniper was a baby and how she would let her sleep on her chest, swaddled and compact, a warm stone. She wouldn't allow herself to fall asleep, afraid she might roll over and crush her daughter in the middle of the night. That was the year she began looking older than her real age, the year of crow's feet and purple circles and her first grays, but she didn't bother covering them, because she wasn't ashamed. Love meant fear, fear meant growing old fast.

᪥

This is what Kaimu lives for now, after years of living for money and lovemaking and the accomplishments of his children: big storms. Or not the storms themselves, but what they wash up on shore, what they knock loose under the sea.

He sits on the porch, listening to the wind pick up, skin tingling at flashes of lightning in the distance. Mai comes out in her nightgown, thin and pale as moonlight, and she asks him what he's doing. There's disapproval in her voice, as there always is when he's up late at night watching storms approach, as there always is when he gets up before dawn to go to the beach and spends hours there, loading his bags with stones and sea glass and shells, wading into the waves with his casting net to drag out more. After, he dumps it all over the garage floor, picking out which pieces to keep for his collection, which to sell to the woman down the street who makes jewelry, which to throw back into the waves.

Kaimu tells his wife he'll be to bed in a few minutes, and she grazes his wrist with her fingertips before going inside, a gesture of tenderness or defeat, Kaimu doesn't know. She's complained to him for years that they don't spend enough time together, says that retirement is the time when they can finally really know one another, but he can't help but feel there's always been something holding him back, with her, with his children, with everyone.

The only one he has ever talked to about the dead girl was his mother, when she was in the hospice losing her memory for good. He'd visit her every day after work, carrying the smell of salt and fish in his hair, and he'd always bring her a present, a little token of something by the sea to keep her company, to make her remember. Of course, she never did—or rather, she remembered wrong, she thought she was back in the Japan of her childhood, thought he was her father. She became obsessed with amber, or what she thought was amber but what he knew was not, since real amber has never been found off their shores. At best, he reasoned, it might be copal, young amber not yet fossilized, but he never told her this. He'd bring her small pieces of it whenever he could, putting them in a porcelain bowl on her bedside table. She was most lucid when rolling the stones in her hands, listening to him recite facts he found for her at the library, useless facts he learned by heart. For instance: amber was made of fossilized resin from an extinct conifer. And: resin oozed from trees where they'd been damaged, like blood from a wound. Resin dropped onto the forest floor and stuck to dirt, sand, clay, insects, bark, moss, feathers, hair. During storms, the sea washed up to the forest and took back with it the resin mixture which would be shaped by waves for years. Some amber is from ninety million years ago. In Japan, the legend is that amber was formed by the setting rays of the sun as they touched the ocean's horizon. Kaimu's mother nodded knowingly at this, as if she remembered. Kaimu would go on and on until it was his mother's bedtime and the nurse ushered him out.

Kaimu raises himself off the rocker, knees creaking, and walks into the garage, rummaging in the dark for his cast net, his backpack, his shovel, his pail. He shakes sand and shell fragments out of his backpack, secures weights to his net. His hands understand these movements in the dark better than they ever understood how to move over his wife's body. He sits, surrounded by tools readied for his morning search. He waits until the first drops of rain cast shadows on the stones, then goes in to try for a few hours of sleep.

꙰

Greta has fallen asleep for two hours—only two hours and already the storm is underway, and she is angry with herself for not waiting up for Juniper. Ray stirs, turns over, mumbles, his voice muffled by the pillow. He asks if she wants him to get up and shut the windows.

"I'll do it," she says, knowing that he knows it's an excuse to make sure Juniper is sleeping soundly in her bed.

She gets up and shuts their window; already the sill is full of water. She kisses Ray on the forehead before leaving the room, tells him she'll probably stay up watching TV, and he grunts his approval, turns over again. She doesn't know how he can sleep through the thunder, but he's always been a heavy sleeper, so healthy and young-looking people sometimes mistake him for her younger brother, a comment that always makes her breath catch in her throat, like a fish stuck on a hook.

She closes the windows in the living room and kitchen, then tiptoes into Juniper's room, careful not to wake her. Juniper has caught Greta a few times standing over her as she sleeps, watching, making sure she's still breathing, and whenever this happens Juniper always gets angry, looks at her like she's been violated in some way.

Juniper is not in her bed.

Greta looks at the clock. Almost two. She peers out the curtains: no car. Lightning flashes, and Greta's heart jolts. In all her years of careful parenting, this is the first time she's lost her daughter. Her mind races through the list of possibilities. Car accident; drinking, pot, coke, speed, heroin, acid, mushrooms, whippits; murdered; robbed; run away; club-hopping with a fake ID; unprotected sex; struck by lightning; hit by a fallen tree; electrocuted by downed power line; drowned in a riptide.

She won't tell Ray, because he'll only try to calm her, and there's nothing more infuriating in these moments of horrible possibilities than someone saying none of them are possible. Anything's possible—that's the most frightening thing about life.

❧

Lately Kaimu has been trying to control his dreams. *Lucid dreaming,* his wife told him, something she learned about in an adult enrichment class she took the year their youngest moved out of the house. Every night before he goes to sleep, he is supposed to write down exactly what he wants to have happen in his dreams, and then when he sleeps he is supposed to become aware that he is dreaming and able to control what happens, to create anything that he wants to happen, as magical or impossible as it might seem. His wife has told him that sometimes in her dreams she flies, other times she talks to her dead parents. He hasn't had such luck; the few times he's become aware that he was dreaming, he felt paralyzed, wasn't even able to move his fingers let alone fly. But he keeps trying.

Tonight, he writes on the slip of paper the same thing that he writes every other night: *I pull girl out of the ocean alive. I save her.*

❧

Greta leaves without telling Ray, without putting on a raincoat, with only sweatpants, sweatshirt, and sneakers, and an umbrella that remains unopened because she is afraid of lightning. The rain is hard, smacks her bare head like tiny, cold eggs, but luckily there's no hail, not yet. Her neighbors' houses are dark, and she imagines them inside, sleeping through the storm, oblivious to the fact that any moment their world might be destroyed, their roofs ripped off, their houses flooded. How nice it would be to be like them, to believe in the benevolence of the world.

When Greta gets to the end of their block, she's not sure which way to go. Few cars cruise the roads at this hour, especially in a storm, but over to her left there is a light still on, a club not yet closed, so she walks in that direction. What are the chances of Juniper being there? Not great, but all Greta knows is that she must keep walking, keep searching or else drown in fear.

The water bubbles up at the gutters and pools around her ankles. Her sneakers are soaked, and when she lifts her feet they feel heavier than ever. She imagines this is how her sister would feel, were she to come back to life: a new heaviness brought on by seawater, her movements slow, staggered, like a creature in a movie they once watched together, *Swamp Thing*, the first and last scary movie Hannah ever saw. This is how Hannah lives with her, still, swimming through her mind even as she searches for her daughter. It's the way Greta preserves her.

Wind tugs at power lines and whistles past dark buildings, pushes against Greta so she has to hold herself up against the vinyl siding of an ice cream shop. When she makes it to the club, she stands outside, face pressed against the window, peering in for any sign of her daughter. A strong gust splays her body against the pane, and inside a man turning away from the bar squints at her, but she's too weak to pry herself from the glass.

Before she has a chance to go inside, she hears her name somewhere beneath the sound of the wind.

She turns around, and there, at the end of the block, is Ray, barefoot, in pajama pants and a T-shirt, completely soaked, their car parked beside him in the road. He trudges toward her, and she's strangely embarrassed, wants to hide. For a moment she wonders how she must look to him, to anyone who might see her: a middle-aged woman, long gray hair dripping down a wet sweatshirt, eyes swollen and red from crying, desperately high-stepping through pools of water in the middle of a near-hurricane to look for her grown daughter.

Ray stops about a foot away from her, as if he knows he can't force her to come back, as if he knows the only way for her to return home would be to ask her and for her to say yes.

Greta braces herself against another gust. She shakes her head no—she has to find Juniper.

Ray grabs her shoulders firmly, seems to resist an urge to shake her. "Gret, she's home."

She looks over at the car, still running, headlights illuminating the rain. Juniper's home. Her legs weaken, unable to hold her waterlogged body. She wants to slip out from between her husband's hands and lie in the near-foot of water, wants to sleep there. A breath heaves out of her lungs, the last wind of a storm.

"She must've gotten home right after you left," Ray says. "She told me she stayed too long at the party and by the time she left she had to drive the long way back to avoid the flooded roads."

Ray takes her arms and leads her to the car. Greta nods, follows. He drives slowly the few blocks to their house, but when they walk up to the porch, she stops at the doorway. She can't go in; she can't face her daughter. She tells Ray she wants to sit on the porch awhile to calm down, and he offers to sit with her.

"I'd rather be alone," she says.

She sees the bathroom light on and knows Juniper must be in there, brushing her teeth.

Ray pauses before going inside and says, "You know, you could've killed yourself tonight."

"I'm sorry," Greta says. She's hot with shame at the thought that Ray and Juniper both caught her at her ugliest, at her most desperate and needy and fearful. She feels like animals do, when they hide in dark corners to die—no one wants to be seen that afraid. That kind of fear is private, more secret than sex.

"You've got to learn to let go," Ray says. "I really thought you were going to try this time."

He shakes his head and walks inside before she has a chance to respond. She wants to tell him she will try harder. But she doesn't know if trying is enough. In the distance, waves glimmer faintly in the dark and crash over the pier, black and shining like the one she stood on years ago, crying for hours, thinking of what to tell her parents after her sister still hadn't returned to the beach blanket and Greta couldn't find her anywhere.

Greta waits on the porch until the storm begins to let up. It's nearly dawn. She takes off her shoes and walks down to the pier.

⅔

The sky is almost clear as Kaimu combs the beach, dragging his casting net behind him, carrying on one shoulder a backpack already half full with shells and stones and sea glass. His pants are rolled up and the detritus is sharp against his feet, a good kind of sharpness that lets him know he's alive, even in a landscape as abandoned as this one, no one on the shore but him and one other person, a woman walking the pier not too far away.

He does not call out to her. Anyone who comes to the beach

at this hour comes for solitude. He drops his backpack on the sand and wades into the sea, up to his shins and then his knees, letting the waves suck him in, breathe him out. He casts the net and lets it unfurl in front of him, weights sinking it so it scrapes the ocean floor, and then he walks backward, pulls it in to shore. Nothing good: broken shells, granite, a dead jellyfish. The storm wasn't as bad as they said it would be, and Kaimu is disappointed with what it has left for him.

He wades in one more time, a little farther, so that he feels the water constrict his chest, cool his blood. He casts the net again, snakes it around on the sea floor, stirring sand and shells.

When he goes to pull it in, the net is stuck, caught on something heavy, and no matter how hard Kaimu tugs, he only succeeds in straining his weak wrists against the resistance of the waves and dragging whatever it is a few inches closer to dry land. Out of the corner of his eye he sees again the woman still pacing the pier. She's within shouting distance, and so he calls to her, asks her to please come help him. Unmoving, she stares at him, and Kaimu regrets having called out. He seems to have frightened her, probably ruined a peaceful moment.

But then she moves down the pier toward shore and trots toward him, calling, "Are you okay? Are you okay?" She rolls up her pants, steps into the water.

Kaimu tells her yes, he's okay, he just needs a hand to drag something out. The waves are strong. As the tide is sucked in, he braces himself against the pull and glimpses something glimmering in his net, a warm color under all the cool grays and greens. He glances back at the woman, and by the way she looks at him he thinks she must have seen it too, and as they watch one another during the silent intake of the tide, Kaimu wonders if he knows this woman, wonders at her secret reason for standing on the pier the morning after a storm.

The woman nods her head. She wades in next to Kaimu and he hands her one side of the net, tells her to simply haul it back to shore as hard as she can. They separate, pulling the net taut, and tug it backward with each wave, struggling against the pull of the sea.

As they get closer to dry sand, Kaimu sees what he has caught. Amber—not copal, he thinks, but the ancient glow of real amber— and it's the largest piece he has ever found, the largest piece he has ever seen, the size of a child's over-inflated beach ball. He wonders, for a moment, if he is dreaming, if this is what happens in lucid dreams, but he knows this is the kind of thing he couldn't make happen even if he tried.

He glances at the woman holding the other end of the net. She's pulling hard against the intake of the tide, her face red and serious, but when she looks at him she laughs, shouts over the waves that she can't believe it, it's beautiful.

In the shallow water the amber glows, a tiny sun rising from the ocean. Kaimu and the woman breathe hard as they haul the stone to shore, and when they finally make it they collapse, tired but happy, as if they've been waiting to do this forever.

ABOUT THE AUTHOR

JACQUELINE VOGTMAN'S FICTION HAS appeared in *Hunger Mountain,
Permafrost, The Literary Review, Smokelong Quarterly, Third Coast,*
and other journals. A graduate of the MFA program at Bowling
Green State University, she is currently Associate Professor of English
at Mercer County Community College. She has lived in New Jersey
most of her life and resides in a small town surrounded by nature,
which she explores with her husband, daughter, and dog. *Girl Country*
is her first book. Find her on Instagram @jacquelinevogtman and
online at jacquelinevogtman.com.

ACKNOWLEDGMENTS

I AM INCREDIBLY GRATEFUL to the whole team at Dzanc for allowing me to share this book with the world. A million thanks to Dan Wickett for choosing my manuscript, and to Michelle Dotter for her smart and insightful edits, which have pushed me to make my stories better in every way. Huge thank you to Steven Seighman for designing a transcendent cover for my book.

This book wouldn't exist without the support of so many teachers throughout the years. Thank you to Mrs. Sebastian and Mrs. Koeller, elementary teachers who allowed me to write my weird little stories; Ms. Wiede, who sent me a book of Li-Young Lee poems in eighth grade; Ms. Morgan, Mrs. Newcomb, Mr. Collins, and Mr. Friedman in high school; Brian Bradford and BJ Ward at WCCC; and Catie Rosemurgy at TCNJ. Special thanks to the Creative Writing MFA program at Bowling Green State University and the brilliant professors I was lucky to spend time with there: Lawrence Coates, Theresa Williams, Mike Czyzniejewski, Karen Craigo, and especially the late great Wendell Mayo, to whom I will be forever grateful.

Thank you to the incredibly talented kindred spirits I was blessed to be in fiction workshop with at BGSU: Catherine, Stephanie, Brandon, Aimee, Meghan, Joe C., Alison, Michelle, and Jessica V., as well as the poets who inspired me there: Callista, Stokely, Jessica S., Brad M., and Laural. Special thanks to those former workshop-mates offering their kind words on this manuscript, whose books have so inspired me: Bess Winter, Brad Felver, Matt Bell, Anne Valente, and Dustin M. Hoffman.

I am thankful for the support of friends old and new; I hope you know that I hold you in my heart always. Thanks as well to my colleagues and students at MCCC, who inspire me daily.

To my family near and far—aunts, uncles, and cousins on the Malloy and Vogtman sides; my siblings' children who are so dear to me; my siblings' partners; my in-laws, the Kinsley-McDonald-Smiley-Tietjen crew—thank you for your encouragement, support, and kinship. I'm grateful, too, for family members who have passed on, especially Opa, whose life story gives me something to aspire to, and Oma and Gran, two of the strongest women I've ever known.

Thanks to my siblings, my best friends, who share with me the most precious thing, childhood: Maura Vogtman, Bridget Quade, Jenny Lumkong, and Dave Vogtman. I love you.

Though he can't read this, I also must thank my most amazing doggo, Teddy, my companion for twelve years and counting, who rested at my feet during the writing of this book.

Mom and Dad, words cannot express the gratitude I hold for you. Thank you for your love, for your stories, for the memories, for inspiring me with a love of nature and books, for believing in me, for putting me through college even when it was difficult, for putting up with me even when I was difficult, for working so hard and allowing me to follow my dreams.

Thank you to Joe, the love of my life for over half my life, for inspiring me and exposing me to music, literature, and film that has shaped my soul. Thank you for being my partner in life and creating life with me. Thank you for your editorial insights on so many of these stories and for being a sounding board for so many wacky ideas. Thank you for working hard for our family, for keeping the house clean, for challenging me, and for looking at the moon with me.

Finally, to my brown-eyed girl, Margot, the heart I carry within my heart: I am so thankful that the universe has given me the opportunity to be your mom. Thank you for your creativity, your sweetness, your curiosity, your love of books, and for allowing me to experience childhood again through your eyes. Thank you for sleeping late some mornings so I could write this book in the pre-dawn silence, but thank you even more for waking up early some days to snuggle beside me, help me with titles, and ask about my stories. You are my sunshine.